D0365806

TO LOVE
A STRANGER

Blythe Bradley

A KISMET® Romance

METEOR PUBLISHING CORPORATION
Bensalem, Pennsylvania

BLYTHE BRADLEY

Blythe Bradley can't remember when she didn't want to write. She has done young adult romances and mysteries as well as adult historicals, mysteries, gothics and family sagas. But, for her, writing romance was the most fun of all. Creating dreams, sharing laughter and tears, finding the secret hearts of special people—it's the gift she gave herself and hopes that you will share.

ONE

Trevor Sinclair lifted his arms, stretching the cramped muscles in his broad shoulders as he leaned back in the oak swivel chair that matched his scarred desk. The afternoon breeze brought the sweet scent of tropical flowers through the open window and he could hear the palm fronds whispering to each other as they stirred. He sighed, frustrated by the piles of papers that littered his desk like an untidy snowfall.

He didn't want to think about his business—it hurt because every deal on which Harlan wanted his opinion reminded him of better times. Not that he blamed Harlan; his best friend and the CEO of ATS Industries was doing a terrific job of covering for him. It was simply that the company and Amanda were forever linked in Trevor's mind.

Trevor rubbed his square chin, which was hidden by the thick black beard he'd grown since his arrival on Bellington Cay. If only he could rub away all the memories, simply erase them from his thoughts and . . . And what would be left? It chilled him to realize that he didn't know.

He'd come to this Caribbean island to get away from the everyday things that reminded him of his wife, to try to heal the wounds Amanda's death had left. But how could he give up the memories of fifteen years of marriage? They'd shared everything, from working together building ATS Industries to enjoying the fruits of its spectacular success. She'd touched every part of his life.

The pain of losing her stabbed at him again. It had been nearly a year since death had ended her suffering and he still couldn't shake the feeling of emptiness. No matter where he went or what he did, life wasn't much fun without Amanda.

"So who said life was supposed to be fun, anyway?" he asked the small yellow and black bird that was hopping along the wooden rail that edged the balcony beyond his window. It paused at the dish of water, silhouetted against the sky, then moved on to the small pile of sugar Trevor had poured out earlier.

Unwilling to dwell on the past, Trevor headed for the French doors that led from his office to the second-floor balcony. The bird watched him, black eyes wary, but it continued to peck at the sugar.

"Getting used to me, aren't you?" Trevor stayed close to the wall of the house as he moved toward the outside staircase that led from the far end of the balcony down to the rank grass that grew between the house and the beach. Six months he'd been on Bellington Cay, having arrived in the muggy heat of summer; now it was November. Tourists were beginning to crowd the island and he was still living like a recluse, seeing few people besides his housekeeper Louise and the occasional lost beachcomber who turned up on his section of sand. No wonder he was talking to the birds.

He raked restless fingers through his already tousled black waves, impatiently pushing the hair out of his eyes. It was time to either get a haircut or find a leather thong to tie his hair back. He grinned, realizing that if he added an eye patch to go with his long hair and beard, he would look enough like a pirate to pose with the tourists. Amanda would laugh herself silly if she could see her proper businessman husband now.

Amanda again. Shaking his head, he hurried down the stairs and headed for the lonely stretch of beach where silky aquamarine waves lapped lazily. His sneakers sank deep in the powdery white sand above the waterline, making running difficult, but he didn't care. The uncertain footing was part of the challenge of jogging on the beach; it claimed his attention, kept him from thinking of much beyond his next step.

Trevor ran until his breath came in rib-stretching gasps that brought a pain knifing into his side. He slowed to a walk, finally willing to admit that he was thirty-eight, not the college track star who'd dreamed of Olympic competition before he'd accepted the practical challenge of the business world.

Sunset had edged nearer as he ran and he was surprised to see a small cluster of lights just ahead. He grinned, suddenly feeling pleased with himself. Maybe he wasn't as decrepit as he thought; after all, he'd just run halfway around the island to the village of Bellington, the only settlement on the cay.

So now what? A beer and a sandwich at the local pub? For a change, that seemed a whole lot more appealing than hiking back to eat the solitary dinner Louise would have left for him. He climbed up from the beach to follow the broken-shell-paved road down the hill into town.

The cooling breeze reminded him that at home winter would be fast approaching. In Denver, Harlan would be waxing his skis and planning, as usual, to spend the Thanksgiving weekend on the snowy slopes of the Rocky Mountains. Another tradition he'd be missing. Trevor quickened his pace along the single paved street of the village, aware of the rising wind as it dried the perspiration on his lean body.

Diana Foster stood before the resort desk staring back at the sad-eyed woman. What the hell was she supposed to do now? Was it her fault her plane had been late getting to Nassau, late enough that she'd missed the single interisland flight from there to Bellington Cay? In fact, her flight had been so late, she'd nearly missed the pokey little ferry that had finally brought her here, which was why she hadn't had time to call and make sure the resort held her reservation.

"I'm sorry, Miss Foster, but there isn't an empty bed in the place. I couldn't hold your room when there were people already waiting to check in." The owner looked genuinely sorry, but that didn't solve Diana's problem.

"Is there any place else you could call?" Diana did her best to keep her tone calm and level, but the rough ferry ride had left her light-headed and far more exhausted than she'd realized.

The woman shook her head. "Bellington has but two resorts and we're both full up for this week and next. The holiday, you know." Her voice had an odd cadence, which might have sounded interesting and exotic under other circumstances.

"But I've no place to go." Only iron-willed self-control kept the words from becoming a wail.

"Well, you might go by the Jolly Roger Pub and talk to the barman there. Joe's related to 'most half the population of the island. Could be he has a cousin or auntie who might rent you a room for a night or two. That's the best I can tell you, unless you'd like to sleep in the lobby here. I'd not turn you out in the damp."

"The Jolly Roger?" Somehow the idea of finding a room at a pub named after a pirate flag didn't sound too appealing, but beggars couldn't be choosers and, at this point, Diana was willing to beg for a place to lie down.

"Right down the street. Likely you passed it on your way from the dock." The woman sounded decidedly eager to have her out of here.

Diana nodded, vaguely recalling music swelling out

of a brightly lit doorway. Her head throbbed and her stomach twisted—just what she needed, a visit to a noisy bar. Gritting her teeth, she picked up her suitcase and headed for the door. This was definitely not an auspicious beginning for what promised to be an incredibly delicate and difficult task.

Don't think about Sinclair now, she warned herself. She'd spent more than enough time stewing about possible approaches to the man while on her long flight from Iowa to Nassau; right now she'd just concentrate on finding a bed. After all, she had a week to figure out how to get the man to resume his neglected duty to support his daughter.

The breeze that had refreshed her when she finally got off the ferry seemed colder now and there were fewer people moving along the village's main street. Since the Jolly Roger was one of the few places showing signs of life, she had no trouble finding it. Still, the mixture of loud music and the myriad food and drink odors that assaulted her when she entered nearly convinced her to accept a night on one of the couches in the resort lobby. Only the realization that most of them were far too short to comfortably accommodate her five-eight frame kept her moving.

Naturally, the place was crowded, the tables mostly filled with laughing groups of what appeared to be tourists. Diana looked around, seeking a corner where she could sit and rest before she tried talking to the barman. Unfortunately, the only empty seats she could see were a couple of stools at the bar—which, the way her luck was running, didn't surprise her at all. Swallowing a sigh, she headed for the one farthest from the jukebox.

Since her suitcase had gained at least fifty pounds on the walk from the resort, she groaned as she dropped it next to the stool, then set her heavy shoulder bag on top of it. The sudden release of weight combined with the warm, smoky air in the pub set her head to spinning so wildly she barely made it up on the stool. She dug her nails into the dark wood of the bar, trying hard to hold onto consciousness.

A muscular arm slipped around her shoulders, steadying her as the room dipped and swayed. "Hey, are you okay?" The male voice was deep and sounded genuinely concerned, but she was too busy trying to stay upright to even look at him or answer.

She couldn't faint. She wasn't the type. This was insane. Diana closed her eyes and clenched her jaws, drawing in a deep, slow breath.

"Would you like a glass of water or something?" The man beside her interrupted her concentration.

Diana managed a weak nod but kept her eyes closed. She didn't think she could handle the dipping and swirling of the lights above the bar. Within seconds, someone was holding a glass to her lips. She pried her nails out of the wood and steadied the glass with one hand. The cool water helped, easing her nausea as well as her dry mouth. She cautiously opened her eyes.

The twinkling lights that were strung along the wall above the bar seemed much less manic now and the stool no longer threatened to buck her off. She focused on the worried face of the black man behind the bar. "You okay, Miss?" he asked. "You ain't gonna faint on us?"

"I've never fainted in my life." Diana tried to straighten up, suddenly very much aware of the heat and strength of the arm supporting her. "I just got a little dizzy."

Her supporter kept his arm where it was, steadying her. "How about something to eat?" he asked, practically speaking into her ear. "Or maybe some fruit juice? A little sugar fix?"

Diana swallowed hard, expecting the mention of food to bring back the nausea that had plagued her on the ferry, but her insides seemed to have settled down now that she was back on dry land. "Maybe some tea and a sandwich?'' She gave the barman more attention, remembering that he was the one she'd come to talk to.

His wide smile probably reflected his relief that she wasn't going to collapse on his floor, but he pointed to a chalkboard that listed the menu of foods available. She selected soup and a chicken sandwich, then braced herself to face the man whose arm was still supporting her. It wasn't that she didn't appreciate his efforts; she simply couldn't let him get the wrong impression just because she'd suffered a moment of weakness.

"I really am all right now," she began. "It was just . . .'' She let it trail off as she got a good look at him. A slightly hysterical giggle rose in her throat. This had to be some kind of crazy nightmare. First she arrived in a place called the Jolly Roger Pub, then she nearly collapsed into the arms of a pirate!

His thick black beard twitched as his lips curved into a grin. She lifted her gaze to meet the most beguiling hazel eyes she'd ever seen. For what seemed an endless interval, she gazed at him while the room, the din, even her own discomfort just faded away; then a shout of laughter from somewhere near the door snapped her back to reality.

She could feel the heat of a blush in her cheeks as she tried to reclaim her tattered dignity. "I do appreciate your help, but I'm fine. The ferry ride was kind of rough and the woman at the resort gave my room away and . . .'' She caught herself, appalled that she'd been babbling her problems to a total stranger. She'd come to the Jolly Roger to ask the barman for his help, not to snuggle up to the most intriguing man she'd ever seen. That thought stiffened her spine.

Trevor released her at once, picking up his beer and taking a long swallow. So she was a tourist. That figured; he sure wouldn't have forgotten a face as striking as the one before him. Her features, framed by an untamed cloud of gold-streaked, tawny hair, were delicate, the prominent cheekbones giving a slight tilt to the wide blue eyes that looked into his. Not the popular concept of beauty, maybe, but definitely far from ordinary.

"You came in on the ferry tonight?" Since he hadn't finished his sandwich yet, it seemed natural to continue the conversation and indulge his curiosity. After all, he had come in here because he didn't want to eat alone, and Joe, the barman, was too busy to be much company tonight.

Diana nodded. "My plane was real late landing in Nassau and I missed my connecting flight here, so I thought it was a good idea. Nobody told me that the stupid boat stopped at every island in this part of the Caribbean."

"You're vacationing alone here?" That surprised him.

Joe arrived with her soup before she could answer and Diana was grateful for the interruption. She wasn't the kind of person who talked to men in bars. She'd always done her best to live up to Mom's description—she was the cautious, dutiful, dependable daughter, the one Mom counted on. At least, she used to be.

An itch of rebellion moved through her as the warm soup renewed her energy. She was twenty-nine years old. Maybe she was entitled to change, to grab a chance at some of the excitement she'd missed growing up. As soon as she'd taken care of Crystal's future . . . She slanted a glance at the pirate, then blushed as she realized that he was still looking at her, waiting for her answer.

The itch expanded into a full-blown longing—why not enjoy herself a little? She gave him the smile his easy grin invited. "Actually, I'm on a sort of business vacation. Something I have to take care of here on the island. But I hope to have time for some fun, too." Her smile ebbed as she remembered her recent encounter at the resort. "Provided, of course, that I can find a place to stay."

"What have you done about that so far?" He was fascinated by the way her every thought and emotion seemed to show in her face. She'd never make a poker player, but she certainly was intriguing to watch.

"The lady at the Bellington Sands called the other resort on the island, but it was full, too. She suggested that I come here and talk to the barman. She seemed to think he might know of someone who'd rent me a room at least for tonight."

The pirate nodded. "Joe might know of someone. In fact, if he doesn't, I could call my housekeeper and ask her. Between them, they know everyone on the island." He took time for a bite of his sandwich, then asked, "What about the business that brought you here? If it's with someone who lives on the cay, they could probably put you up for the night."

Diana nearly choked on her soup, the very suggestion causing her throat to close. She had to swallow twice before she felt safe in speaking. "I don't think that would be a good idea."

Her adamant tone told him there was more to this business vacation than met the eye. Trevor found himself grinning. A lady of mystery stranded on Bellington? The thought intrigued him, so he decided to see what he could find out. "I can't imagine anyone refusing you shelter, Miss . . . ?"

"Diana Foster." Diana answered, realizing that they'd never taken time to introduce themselves. "And you're . . . ?"

"Trevor Sinclair at your service."

Diana was too stunned to even notice the clatter as she dropped her spoon into her bowl. This was Trevor Sinclair? Her mind rebelled at the idea that her friendly pirate could be the man she'd come so far to see. She tried to match the face before her with the dreamy-eyed descriptions of him she'd heard from her sister; but, of course, eighteen years of living and a sexy black beard would have changed the face, and time had definitely blurred her memories.

"Is something wrong?" Trevor took her hand, surprised at how cold her fingers were. "Are you feeling ill again?"

For a heartbeat, she considered faking a faint. Or maybe she wouldn't need to fake it. This day had brought her enough shocks to cause a real faint. Unless, of course, she was going to be saved from this nightmare by the alarm clock. She closed her eyes, hoping that when she opened them, she'd be back in Pleasant Valley, Iowa.

"Talk to me, lady." His tone was demanding, forcing her back to reality. "Tell me what's wrong."

Diana took a deep breath, facing the fact that she wasn't going to wake up safe in her own bed. So what was she going to do? She couldn't just blurt out the reason for her visit to the island—not here, not now. But she couldn't just get up and walk away, either, especially since she had nowhere to go.

"I'm sorry, I guess it just caught up with me again. I mean, it's been an incredibly long day and then to get here and find out that I have no room reserved and . . ." She let it trail off, forcing a smile she was far from feeling. He was holding her hand! In her shock, she hadn't even noticed. Now her fingers were tingling from his touch.

"Why don't you let me take you to my house? I'm sure you'll feel better after a good night's sleep and . . ." He let it trail off as he recognized something very much akin to fear in her eyes.

"Stay with you?" She was embarrassed by the way her voice squeaked, but she couldn't help it. She stole a glance at him, trying to read his expression. He appeared slightly perplexed, but she could also see concern in his face. He looked exactly like a nice man who was worried about a stranger.

Which he was, she realized, the tremors of shock

fading from her mind. Of course, there was no reason for him to recognize her, since he'd never seen her, nor would he know her by the name Foster. For a moment, she wondered what he would have said if she'd introduced herself as Diana Johnson. Then she dismissed the idea—he probably wouldn't have recognized that name either. A man who could forget his own daughter surely wouldn't recall the name of his lover's sister.

"What do you have against my offer?" Trevor released her hand, doing his best to hide his irritation at her odd reaction to his invitation. "I realize that you don't know me, but as I recall, you came in here to ask Joe about renting a room somewhere. Wouldn't that mean staying with a total stranger?"

She was forced to nod since she couldn't explain that her initial reaction had come precisely because he wasn't a total stranger. At least his name wasn't strange to her.

He pressed on. "And if Joe had offered to find you a place, wouldn't you have accepted it?"

"I suppose so." Damn, but his logic was hard to dispute. Or perhaps she was feeling less like disputing it. "It's just that I didn't want you to think . . ." She stopped, aware that she was going to sound rather naive. "I would have been asking him because the woman at the resort suggested that he might know of some lady . . ."

Trevor swallowed a chuckle, suddenly aware of how his offer must appear to her. She thought he was hitting on her! He didn't know whether to be flattered or insulted. Probably better to be neither—at least if he wanted her to accept his help. And, though he wasn't sure why, that was what he wanted. Assuming a serious expression, he decided to try a new tack.

He called Joe over. "Miss Foster is looking for a room for the night, Joe. Do you know of anyone with an extra bed?"

The barman frowned, then shook his head. "I doubt there's an extra bed to be had on the island tonight, thanks to that planeload of folks who got stranded on their flight from Pine Isle. I know Aunt Louise took in a couple and so did my cousin Carrie." He offered Diana an apologetic smile as a call came from the other end of the bar. "I'm real sorry, ma'am."

Diana swallowed hard. Somehow she hadn't expected such a quick answer to her question—especially not a negative one. Joe the barman was supposed to call around and find her a bed, so she could escape this din and find enough peace and quiet to figure out if this Trevor Sinclair and the man she'd come to confront could be the same person.

"I have a large house, Miss Foster, and I frequently have friends or business acquaintances staying over with me. I can assure you that your reputation will in no way be endangered by your accepting my invitation. As you heard from Joe, there are plenty of other visitors to our island staying in private homes. When you live on an island, you help people out."

Diana forced herself to meet his gaze, carefully considering his words. Would she have accepted the invitation from the kindly pirate if he hadn't turned out to be Trevor Sinclair? Honesty forced her to admit that she certainly would have been tempted.

The barman returned with her sandwich. "I asked a coupla fellas and they already rented out their spare rooms, Miss. There's just nuthin' left, I'm sorry." He shook his head. "I dunno what to suggest."

"Thank you for trying." Diana managed a weak smile, visions of the uncomfortable furniture at the resort filling her mind.

Trevor waited until Joe left. "Looks like you're stuck with me, Miss Foster. Unless you plan on sleeping in the lobby of one of the resorts." He didn't bother saying he was sorry since he wasn't. His curiosity about the woman grew stronger every minute he was with her.

"I hate to impose, Mr. Sinclair."

"Why don't you call me Trevor since you're going to be my houseguest?" His easy grin oozed charm.

"If you'll call me Diana." She couldn't help responding to him. "And I really do appreciate your kindness, Trevor. It has been a very long day."

"In that case, why don't you eat your sandwich while I call Eban? He owns the island taxi. I jogged into town this evening and it would be a pretty long hike back to my house carrying a suitcase."

To his house. The words and the intimacy they implied sent a quiver through her. Nerves or anticipation? She wasn't sure she even wanted to know. When she'd decided to make the long flight from Iowa to the Caribbean to talk to Trevor Sinclair, she'd certainly never considered the possibility that meeting Crystal's father might be anything but an ordeal. Never in her wildest dreams had she envisioned herself staying in his house.

It was barely twenty minutes later when Trevor waved to an elderly man who appeared in the doorway of the pub, then escorted her to the ancient and battered sedan parked outside. Diana hugged her overstuffed shoulder bag to her chest as she settled on the worn seat. "This is a taxi?" she murmured, sure that the driver couldn't hear her over the clatter of the engine.

"It beats walking." Trevor shivered, cold in his shorts and light knit shirt. "Besides, that wind feels like there's a storm brewing."

Diana shivered, too, though more from uneasiness than the cold. The moment they left the paved street, the shadows seemed to absorb the feeble rays of the car's headlights. The rattling taxi bounced wildly along what appeared to be a rutted path between thick groves of trees or bushes.

"Where exactly do you live?" Diana asked as they

crossed an open grassy area, then plunged into another stand of trees.

"On the south end of the island. The town is on the northern tip. It's not much farther." Trevor sounded amused, probably because he could hear the nervous quiver in her voice.

Diana straightened her spine and released her stranglehold on the shoulder bag. So she was basically a small-town girl. That didn't mean she couldn't handle a sophisticated man like Trevor Sinclair. Right was on her side—and Crystal's; all she had to do was make him see that.

"The house is up ahead." Trevor interrupted her thoughts as the car bucked under the onslaught of the rising wind. A lone two-story house rose ahead, pale against the dark sky and the restless sea.

Diana swallowed hard as she got out of the taxi. Naturally, Trevor Sinclair couldn't live on a friendly street like an ordinary person—he had to have his place out in the middle of nowhere. She gasped as she realized that the house was totally dark. Surely he didn't expect her to stay out here alone with him! She opened her mouth to object, but the taxi was already heading back along the road.

"I'm sorry the place looks so dark and deserted, but it was still daylight when I went out for my run and I expected to be home long before this." Trevor tried for a reassuring note as he sensed her apprehension.

"You live out here alone?" She did her best to keep her nervousness from showing in her voice. Where were the herds of servants she'd imagined now that she needed them?

"It's really not that far from the village. My housekeeper Louise usually walks to and from town. I rarely use my car except when I have to pick up supplies or meet friends at the airstrip." He cupped her elbow with a friendly hand, urging her along the front walk before she took off at a dead run. His mystery lady was also amazingly skittish. He couldn't help wondering why.

He opened the unlocked front door. "Come on in and sit down, Diana. I'll get a fire started and warm the place up."

She blinked, nearly blinded by the light after the darkness. The huge living room they'd entered was re-assuringly ordinary with its collection of comfortable overstuffed furniture. As near as she could tell, the room took about half the width of the house, ending in a partial wall that held an elaborate collection of entertainment equipment. Beyond the arch in the dividing wall, she could see dining room furniture.

Still apprehensive, she stayed near the door as Trevor crossed to the large stone fireplace that dominated the far end of the room. "This won't take long." He knelt down to ignite the carefully arranged logs. Almost at once, friendly crackling sounds filled the air with the promise of warmth. "Now, isn't that better?"

Diana moved toward the fireplace, drawn as much by his smile as by the cheery fire. He certainly didn't seem predatory. Not that she was a great judge of men's intentions—as Ken Foster had proved. She pushed that thought away firmly. This was no time to dwell on her past mistakes.

Trevor stepped back from the fireplace, pleased to see the tension easing from her expression. Maybe if he gave her a few minutes alone, she'd relax again. "I'll just plug in the coffeepot before I go up and change into something a little warmer, then we can get acquainted."

Diana nodded, watching with interest as he disappeared into the kitchen, then returned to run lightly up the graceful wrought-iron staircase that led from near the kitchen doorway to the second floor. For a man at least two inches over six feet, he moved with the grace of a cat. And the well-muscled legs revealed by his dark green Bermuda shorts certainly looked as though they belonged to an athlete, not a desk-bound businessman.

So who was Trevor Sinclair? She had trouble picturing the gentle pirate she'd met as the mysterious lover who'd broken her sister Eileen's heart or the unfeeling monster that her mother still cursed from time to time. She moved closer to the fire, wishing there were answers in the dancing flames.

She shivered as a blast of wind rattled the door and hurled rain against the windows. Could she simply be seeing what she wanted to see when she looked at Trevor? He was handsome and charming, there was no doubt about that. So where did that leave her? The answer was chilling. She was the houseguest of a man cruel and unfeeling enough to refuse to see or hear anything about his child. Yet he was the same man who had faithfully supported that child for fifteen years.

Hugging herself, she moved to the couch that had been pulled up close to the hearth. The soft avocado velvet welcomed her as did the warmth of the fire. She slipped off her shoes and tucked her cold toes under her.

She was much too tired to sort everything out now, she decided. Figuring out what Trevor Sinclair was really like was a job for someone with a clear mind and, at the moment, her headache was returning. Making Crystal's dreams a reality would just have to wait until tomorrow. Right now all she wanted to do was curl up and close her eyes for a few minutes.

TWO

Trevor paused at the top of the stairs, feeling much more comfortable now that he'd pulled on a pair of dark brown cords and a lightweight gold sweater. He'd gotten used to the casual island life-style, but Diana's obvious uneasiness about being here alone with him made him sure she'd feel better with a properly dressed host.

Now where the heck had she disappeared to? He relaxed as he caught a glimpse of burnished golden brown hair over the back of the couch nearest the fireplace. She must be lying down. He cleared his throat, wanting her to know that he was coming, so he wouldn't startle her. She didn't move even as he clattered down the metal steps.

He hurried to the couch, remembering all too well her spell of dizziness when she'd first entered the pub. She'd said it was just exhaustion and the strain of her trip, but . . . His worry faded as he looked down at her. Diana's eyes were closed, her expression peaceful; her slow, deep breathing made it clear that she was sound asleep. Trevor relaxed. Jet lag he could understand. There'd been times when he and Amanda . . .

He stiffened, suddenly realizing that he hadn't thought

about Amanda for hours. For a moment he nearly surrendered to the sharp sting of guilt, then the logical part of his mind banished it. He'd gone out running to escape the haunting memories, so why should he feel guilty for succeeding? Maybe meeting the mysterious Diana Foster was just the distraction he needed.

He certainly enjoyed watching her sleep. Her soft, full lips, slightly parted now, were inviting and her thick, dark eyelashes lay like heavy shadows on her pale cheeks. Actually, there was something oddly familiar about her profile, the sweep of her cheekbones and the line of her elegant nose, but he couldn't seem to place where he might have seen her.

It had to have been a photograph, perhaps in a magazine. He was sure he wouldn't have forgotten her, if they'd ever been introduced. Diana Foster was an impressive woman. And a tempting one; he had to fight an urge to smooth back the tangled curls that spilled around her face.

Surprised by his reaction, he stepped back from the couch. What the devil was he doing mooning over his sleeping houseguest? What he needed was a cup of coffee and a strong dose of reality, not an erotic fantasy about Diana Foster. In fact, he should be deciding how to awaken her so he could get her off the couch and upstairs to one of his guest rooms.

In the kitchen, Trevor poured himself a mug of coffee, then leaned against the counter as he contemplated what he'd done. Bringing home a pretty stranger was definitely a first for him. He grinned. At least it fit in with his new image—the pirates he remembered from the movies were always bringing home lovely young captives. Not that Diana could be considered a captive.

Shaking his head at his own fanciful thoughts, he opened the refrigerator. Maybe if he fed her something . . . He spotted a plate of Louise's cinnamon rolls. Warmed in the microwave, they should be perfect for a cold, rainy night. He chuckled. He'd always maintained that the aroma of those rolls would raise the dead and Diana was certainly dead to the world.

Diana stirred. She was at home in Pleasant Valley. Mom was doing her Saturday baking, filling the house with the wonderful scents of rolls and cookies, bread and cake. Dad was still alive, working too hard; but he'd be home soon and . . . She opened her eyes just in time to see a man setting a tray on the table beside the couch where she was lying.

"Have a nice nap?" His gentle grin eased away her momentary flash of apprehension.

Slightly disoriented, she smiled back. Where the heck was she? The room was . . . Memories crowded into her mind and her feeling of ease vanished. She was in Trevor Sinclair's house. She'd fallen asleep on his couch and now he was offering her coffee and what smelled suspiciously like cinnamon rolls, one of her larger weaknesses.

Embarrassed, she struggled to sit up, seeking with her toes the shoes she'd kicked off. "I'm sorry, Trevor, I just meant to close my eyes for a moment, but . . ."

His chuckle was warm and intimate as a caress. "Don't apologize, Diana. You told me you were exhausted. I should have just shown you up to your room. I am familiar with jet lag, when we used to travel for the company . . ." He stopped, his grin seeming to congeal as he suddenly focused his attention on the tray. "Would you like a roll and some coffee? I promise I won't keep you up much longer."

"They look wonderful. In fact, I was dreaming about the ones Mom used to bake. Must have been the aroma." To cover her discomfort, Diana accepted one of the sticky rolls and the mug of coffee.

Trevor watched her, sensing her relaxation as he told her about Louise and her love of baking. Diana hadn't slept long, but she definitely looked better now, less edgy. His curiosity about her returned. He decided to see if she was ready to answer a few questions. "So will you be spending your whole vacation on Bellington Cay, or is this just your first stop?"

Her coffee sloshed slightly as her hand jerked, but when she met his gaze, her smile was still in place. Only now it didn't reach her dark blue eyes and he could almost feel the tension in her slender body. Not exactly the reaction he'd expected.

"I really haven't made any concrete plans." Diana spoke quickly, trying hard to cover her uneasiness. "My coming here was sort of spur of the moment." That much was true enough. In fact, she had a feeling she should have given the whole idea a bit more thought and study before she hopped on the plane. "And, of course, my plans will depend on whether or not I can find a place to stay."

A spur of the moment business vacation? That made no sense, especially since she seemed most reluctant to talk about whom she'd come to see. In fact, he was more than a little suspicious about her motives for coming here; but since access to Bellington Cay was limited, he knew he'd have plenty of time to indulge his curiosity. "Well, you're welcome to stay here for as long as you like. As you can see, I have plenty of room."

Such generosity. She would have been more impressed if she hadn't wondered why he was being so nice. Bitter experience had taught her that men rarely offered a woman such kindness without expecting something in return. So maybe if she asked the right questions, she'd find out enough about him to figure out what he might want from her. "Your home is lovely. Have you been here long?"

"Six months." Thoughts of the reasons for his coming here momentarily derailed his curiosity about Diana.

"Surely you're not . . . ah . . . retired?" Or maybe hiding out from creditors? She suddenly wished she'd asked her mother's banker about the financial condition of Sinclair, Inc., when she'd questioned him about the lack of money in Crystal's trust account. In the few days since she'd learned that the checks had stopped being deposited almost two full years ago, she'd come up with a number of possible reasons for Trevor Sinclair's neglect of his daughter; but she'd never . . .

"Of course not. I find it easy to keep in touch with my company from here." The sharpness of his tone told her that he resented her question.

"I just thought you were much too young to . . ." She let it trail off, wishing she'd remembered to keep her mouth shut. For a person who'd always prided herself on being cautious, she was showing a surprisingly impulsive streak. Which she might live to regret. All she needed now was for him to get suspicious and chuck her out in the storm.

She looked so upset by his response to her question, Trevor took pity on her by changing the subject. "Would you like more coffee? There's plenty in the kitchen."

More coffee and more questions? Diana knew she couldn't handle the strain, not tonight. "I think I'd rather skip the second cup of coffee and put my weary head on a pillow, if you don't mind. The roll was wonderful, but I'm pretty much out of it now."

Better to beat a retreat while she still had the promise of a place to sleep. Tomorrow she'd be in much better shape to decide how to broach the subject of Crystal's future to the stranger she'd come so far to confront. Right now she just couldn't seem to hate the friendly pirate the way she knew she should hate the man who'd ruined her sister's life and cared for Crystal only with his checkbook.

"Where in the world did you fly to Bellington from—the West Coast?"

"Iowa. And to be honest, I feel like my flight took off at least a week ago." She got slowly to her feet, half expecting to be as dizzy as she'd been in the pub. This time, however, the room remained stable. "If you'll point me in the direction of your guest room, I promise to be more coherent tomorrow."

Trevor studied her expression for a moment, then got to his feet. He could tell from the look in her eyes that he wouldn't learn anything more about his mysterious guest tonight. "You have a choice, since I have two guest rooms; but I'd recommend the one that faces the back of the house. It has the ocean view."

"Sounds perfect." She picked up her shoulder bag and followed him up the wrought-iron staircase, suddenly feeling uncomfortable again. The house seemed to echo with emptiness as he opened the bedroom door and switched on the lights.

Shivers traced down her spine as he placed her suitcase on the bed and crossed to open the door of a small bathroom. "The bath connects to the other guest room, so you can check it out. If you need anything, let me know. I'll be downstairs for a while. Otherwise, I'll see you in the morning."

"Thank you, Trevor." She stiffened as he brushed past her; for some reason, he seemed much bigger now than he had when they'd been sitting downstairs. Or maybe the room was smaller. Or she was losing it.

She stood very still until she heard him clattering down the stairs, then slumped on the bed beside her suitcase. What was she doing here? What madness had prompted her to accept his invitation after he'd introduced himself?

She smiled wryly as she pushed her hair back. If she remembered correctly, her acceptance had something to do with short resort couches and a romantic pirate with kind eyes. Or jet lag. She shook her head. Or maybe she really was going crazy.

In the few days since she'd discovered that there wasn't enough money in Crystal's account for her to accept the opening she'd been offered at the prestigious

Wilding School of Music, nothing she'd done had made much sense. Unfortunately, she couldn't see that she'd had much choice. Crystal had suffered enough through the years because she didn't have a father in her life; there was no way Diana could let her be deprived of the education her talent deserved.

Sobered and strengthened by that thought, Diana began to unpack. Maybe she'd done the right thing, accepting Trevor's invitation. Now that she was here under his roof, she'd have a chance to get to know him as a person before she asked him for the money. The fact that her heartbeat quickened at the prospect of getting to know him meant nothing at all. Still, she couldn't help thinking that this mission would have been much less complicated if he'd been the typical spoiled rich man she'd expected. Somehow his buccaneer's charm had a way of confusing her.

She caught her lower lip between her teeth. She couldn't let his appeal sidetrack her, not now. Since she had no job and little prospect of finding one before the first of the year, she couldn't help Crystal financially and with Mom's health problems forcing her to sell the shop in Pleasant Valley . . .

Diana lifted her chin, forcing her family's financial problems from her mind. What she needed to do now was unpack a nightgown and get some sleep. She'd definitely need all her wits about her tomorrow when she started asking Trevor some of the questions that had tormented her through the years. Like why he'd refused to marry Eileen once Eileen discovered she was pregnant with his child.

Thinking of Eileen sent her spirits plummeting again. She'd always adored her big sister, but she'd never understood her; not while they were growing up and not through the years after Eileen came back to Pleasant Valley with her baby. Diana smiled, thinking of Crystal, the real live doll that Diana had come to feel was as much her baby as Eileen's.

Not wanting to get lost in her memories, Diana finished her unpacking, donned a nightgown, and slipped between sheets that smelled of sunshine. She was asleep almost as soon as she closed her eyes.

Trevor moved restlessly around the living room, paused to study his collection of videotapes, then shifted his attention to the compact discs. Nothing caught his interest, yet he was still too wired to go to bed. He grinned. He couldn't remember the last time he'd felt this need for action. If it hadn't been for the woman sleeping in the room next to his office, he'd have gone up and tackled the pile of paperwork on his desk.

Ah, yes, the woman. He settled on the couch by the fire, relaxing against the soft cushions, picturing Diana in his mind, haunted by the feeling that he'd seen her before. Or maybe someone who looked a lot like her. He shook his head, amused at his own curiosity. Nothing like a little mystery to liven up his life.

Maybe Harlan was right. Every phone call, he insisted that it was time Trevor quit hiding out on the island. Until now, though, he hadn't paid much attention, but tonight . . . For the first time in months, he really missed the challenge of the business world, the old excitement of running ATS Industries.

Could a stranger have made such a difference in the way he looked at the future? Or had he finally just reached a point in his grief where he was ready to try going on with his life? The only answer was a muffled thud as a log settled on the hearth and the hard rattle of windblown rain against the window. His restlessness ebbed, leaving weariness.

As he climbed the stairs, Trevor was sure of only one thing—his heart was lighter tonight than it had been in months. Whatever the future held for him, he was definitely looking forward to spending tomorrow learning everything he could about Diana and her mysterious business vacation.

Diana twisted on the hard mattress, trying to escape the nightmare that seemed to be closing in on her. Ken's familiar features filled her mind—not the dignified, smiling face he showed to the world, but one twisted by cold fury. "You'll be sorry, Diana. I won't let you embarrass me this way. You're my wife and you'll not destroy everything I've worked so hard to create for both of us." He shook her violently, his fingers biting into the soft flesh of her arms. "You hear me? I won't let you ruin everything!"

Diana sat up, gasping as bright sunlight nearly blinded her. Where was she? For a moment, she didn't recognize anything, then her panic ebbed and memories of yesterday filtered into her mind. It wasn't Ken Foster's anger she had to fear, she realized; it was Trevor Sinclair's.

Momentarily overwhelmed at the prospect, she considered putting her head under the pillow and going back to sleep; but the nightmare had made that escape unappealing. Sighing, she glanced at her watch and gasped. Nine-thirty! The morning was half gone and she still hadn't a clue as to how to tell Trevor who she really was, let alone why she'd come.

Shaking her head, she slipped on her robe, picked up the clothes she'd laid out last night, and headed for the bathroom to take a shower. Since when had her life turned into a soap opera? The answer was straight out of her nightmare—things had begun to go wrong the day she'd realized that the man she'd married wasn't anything like the wonderful man she'd fallen in love with. And nothing much had gone right since.

The familiar feeling of defeat swept over her. She had married with such high hopes, been so proud to be the bride of the elegantly handsome and distinguished principal of Cliffton School for Girls. After all, Ken

Foster had been her mentor from the moment he took over running the boarding school where she taught high school English and acted as school librarian.

His courtship had been slow and romantic, tender and very proper, so different from her few brushes with burning passion in college. She'd listened breathlessly to his plans and dreams for their future together. Because he was so positive that they were meant for each other, she'd ignored the lack of fireworks between them. She'd let him take charge of her life until one day, after about six months of marriage, she'd realized that she didn't have a life of her own and she didn't belong in the one Ken insisted was perfect for her.

But that was ancient history. Diana lifted her face to the stinging spray. The divorce had been unpleasant, but it was over and now she had a chance to make a new life for herself. Or she would have once she got Crystal's future settled. Which brought her back to why she was here. She turned off the shower, her determination returning. She could do it, she had to!

Trevor heard her coming down the stairs as he poured his second cup of coffee. So she was finally going to join him; it was about time. It seemed hours since he'd heard the shower running and his curiosity was growing by leaps and bounds. After spending half the night wondering about her, he still couldn't figure out what kind of business could have brought a stunning woman like Diana to Bellington Cay.

Not that he had any intention of just asking her point-blank, he reminded himself as he opened the refrigerator. He didn't want her freezing up on him again the way she had last night. At least, he thought it was his question about who she'd come to see that had changed her mood. He'd hate to think it was hearing his name that had caused her dizzy spell.

He glared into the refrigerator, wondering what she'd want to eat. Since they'd polished off the last of Louise's cinnamon rolls last night, he got out the English muffins and poured her a glass of orange juice. If she liked a big breakfast, he had eggs and there was probably some ham or bacon in the freezer. Louise never left him without the basic necessities.

Trevor caught his breath as Diana came through the kitchen doorway. Her slim white slacks and blue and white cotton sweater gave him an excellent view of her elegantly long legs and nicely rounded curves. Gone was the tense, weary woman who'd fallen asleep on his couch; this Diana fairly glowed with vitality and energy. Still, when she met his eyes, he sensed reservations behind her bright smile and sparkling eyes.

"Good morning, Trevor. I'm sorry I overslept. I hope I haven't kept you from . . ." Diana let it trail off, suddenly uncomfortable with the breezy tone she'd decided was best suited to the occasion. Casual didn't quite mesh with a pulse rate gone mad at the sight of him in his soft tan cotton pants and a body-molding red knit shirt. The man had no business being a hunk. She couldn't deal with rampant hormones now; she had to concentrate on Crystal's needs.

"Good morning to you and don't worry, I haven't been up that long either." Mostly because he'd lain awake half the night fantasizing about her like some bloody teenager. He forced some of the more entertaining scenarios from his mind. "Would you like some coffee? Maybe an English muffin or two?"

"Just one muffin, please, and coffee sounds heavenly." The intimacy of the setting added to her discomfort as she accepted a tall glass of juice and sat down at the small kitchen table. Somehow broaching the reasons for her visit to Bellington Cay had seemed a lot easier while she was rehearsing her arguments in front of the mirror. Just looking into Trevor's sinfully sexy eyes turned her resolve to mush.

"So are you feeling better today?" Not that he couldn't tell just looking at her, but he wanted to start a conversation and that seemed like a reasonable way to begin.

"Much, thank you. I really appreciate the room. I'm not sure I would have survived the resort lobby." She fought an urge to flirt with him, reminding herself that she'd come here for a serious purpose, but after a moment, she reconsidered. Maybe it would be a mistake to plunge right into her reasons for seeking him out. What would be the harm in getting to know more about him first?

Besides, there were other things to consider. Like what she was going to tell Crystal when she got home. Though her niece insisted that she had no interest in the man who'd given her life, Diana wasn't fooled. Crystal had to be intensely curious about her father, not to mention especially vulnerable, since her mother's death nearly six years ago.

"Would you prefer peach jam or grape jelly?" Trevor's casual question snapped her attention back to the present and she realized that her English muffin was now toasted.

"Peach, I guess." She gave him a quick smile, then focused on spreading butter and jam on the muffin. For some reason, she was having a hard time meeting his curious gaze. Maybe because she felt a little guilty about her charade? She'd never been one to play games with the truth.

But why should she worry about being honorable? This was the man who'd left Eileen pregnant and unmarried, ruining her life and cheating his daughter out of everything that should have been hers. He was the one who'd promised money on the condition that he never hear about his child. A man like that . . .

"So what would you like to do today?" Trevor derailed her dark thoughts, forcing her to look up at him.

"Do?" She met his friendly gaze and almost shook her head. He couldn't be the evil man her mother had ranted about through the years. "I hadn't really thought

. . ." She was flunking elementary conversation, but then he had an advantage. She needed a minimum of two cups of coffee to bring her brain up to speed and she'd barely started on her first.

"Well, I'd be happy to show you the island, if you're interested. Or you're welcome to just bask on my beach now that the storm is over." Trevor hesitated a moment, still a little confused by the conflicting signals he seemed to be getting from her. One minute he thought she was getting friendly, the next she was freezing up. Could she be worrying about this mysterious business that had brought her to the cay? He decided to give her an opening to tell him about it. "Unless you're in a hurry to take care of the business that brought you here?"

Diana met his gaze, trying to read his mood, and felt herself melting. He was obviously curious, but he also looked as though he meant the invitation. He was irresistible. "My business can wait." She ignored her inner-warning voice, the one that always sounded suspiciously like her mother. "I'd love to see the island and lying on the beach sounds wonderful, too. I just don't want to be a bother . . ."

"There's nothing on my desk that can't wait." Trevor got to his feet. "I talked to Louise earlier; told her not to worry about getting out here early today, since Joe said she'd taken in a couple of stranded people. Why don't I call her now and see if she'll fix us a picnic lunch? We can pick it up on our way around the island. Unless you'd rather eat lunch at one of the resorts?"

"A picnic sounds perfect." Diana found his enthusiasm endearing and his eagerness to please her totally unexpected. Somehow, she'd always pictured him as super-sophisticated and far too jaded to enjoy simple pleasures. In fact, she had to admit, there was nothing about this Trevor Sinclair that fit the images she'd formed through the years as she listened to Mom and Eileen cussing and discussing him.

Sobered by that realization, she tried to concentrate on her food while Trevor made his phone call, but the friendly way he teased his housekeeper just added to the confusion that had begun the moment he'd told her his name. Could the past eighteen years have changed him so much, or was there a dark side to Trevor, one that she hadn't yet seen?

That thought knotted her stomach. She'd been so easily fooled by Ken's charming public personality, never guessing that he could be vicious when crossed. Learning the truth about him had been shockingly painful and was a lesson she'd never forget. Which meant that getting to know Trevor before she told him who she was might be the best way to protect Crystal. If he was hiding a cruel side, she certainly didn't want to risk exposing the fragile seventeen-year-old to the kind of pain a second rejection by her father would inflict.

She'd have to be careful, Diana decided, frowning at the beautiful view of aquamarine water and pale sand that stretched beyond the open kitchen door. If Crystal lost her opportunity to study at the Wilding School of Music because there was no money for her tuition, that would hurt her, but she'd recover from the disappointment. Facing an uncaring father would be devastating. For the first time, Diana regretted the impulse that had led her to tell Crystal why she was making the trip to Bellington Cay.

Trevor watched the play of emotions as they moved over Diana's expressive features. What the heck was bugging her now? When he'd first suggested the picnic, she'd been as enthusiastic as a little kid, but now her midnight blue eyes had a brooding look. Was she having second thoughts about spending the day with him? He was surprised at how much that idea bothered him.

Seeking a way to bring back her enthusiasm, he

asked, "So, Diana, shall we take the car or walk on our tour of the island?"

"What?" Diana blinked at him, trapped for a moment in her own worries, then the concern in his gaze registered and she realized that she was being rude. "I'm sorry, I was thinking about some problems at home and . . ." She let it trail off, wondering what in the world had prompted that little confession. She forced a chuckle. "Isn't that always the way? You go on vacation to get away from things, then worry about them instead of having fun."

Trevor nodded, suddenly aware that he might be using her presence here as a diversion from his own problems. "If you'll give me a chance, I'll do my best to help you forget your troubles entirely."

"I think I'd like that." She couldn't help responding to his sexy grin, and when she looked deep into his eyes, she found it very easy to forget anything beyond the moment.

"So do you want a walking or riding tour?" He felt tingling sparks of excitement coursing through his veins as he looked into her eyes. He hadn't felt so truly alive for months.

"Walking, I think, if it isn't terribly far."

"The island's only a couple of miles long by about a mile wide. Of course, following the coastline is longer, but we can always have Eban bring us home if you're tired after our picnic."

"What makes you think I'll be the one who gets tired?" She couldn't resist teasing him. "I'm used to jogging four or five miles every other day—or I was before the weather back home turned so cold."

"That's what I was doing last night, running on the beach."

"This must be a heavenly place to run." Diana looked wistfully at the beach. "I get so bored going around the same streets at home and it wasn't much better at the school, except that I had access to the indoor track in the winter."

"School?" Trevor frowned. Could she be a college student? He'd judged her to be in her late twenties, but then she could be getting an advanced degree.

"The Cliffton School for Girls. I taught high school English and served as school librarian there until this past spring."

"You're a high school teacher?" He was too surprised to hide it. He'd given quite a bit of thought to her possible profession, finally deciding that, with her exotic looks, she might be a model. One place he hadn't pictured her was in a schoolroom.

"It's a tough job, but someone has to do it." Her soft chuckle spoke of good memories. "And I do love it." Her happy look faded as a flicker of something very like longing crossed her face, then vanished as she gave him a smile that didn't quite dispel the sadness in her eyes. "But I'm on vacation now, so let's not talk about work. I want to hear more about this tour we're going on."

"Well, now, why should we talk, when we could be on our way? Unless you'd like something more to eat?" Trevor noted her odd reaction to talking about her profession but decided against asking any questions. She was right—whatever was troubling her could wait. Right now the sunlight beckoned, offering what he needed most—escape to a world of laughter and fun.

THREE

"How much farther did you say it was to Hibiscus Cove?" Diana stopped to empty the small stones out of her sandals for the fourth time since they'd left the main path.

"Getting tired?" Trevor's solicitous tone didn't quite disguise the amusement in his eyes.

"Only of emptying out stones," Diana lied, smiling bravely. She was definitely regretting her crack about him being the one who'd get tired first. But how was she to know he could walk a horse into the ground? Too late she'd remembered her glimpse of his well-muscled legs as he'd climbed the stairs last night. "Besides, I am getting hungry." She directed her gaze hopefully toward the hamper they'd picked up earlier. After all, it was nearly two o'clock.

"The cove is just around that clump of trees up ahead." Trevor had the grace to look guilty. "I think you'll find it worth the walk and, with any luck, we'll have it to ourselves. The tourists never seem to wander this far from town."

Probably because the tourists had the good sense to just enjoy themselves on the beautiful stretches of beach Trevor had insisted they bypass, Diana thought bitterly.

She, for one, would have been happy to stop at any of them. She would be happy to stop, period.

Trevor halted as soon as he rounded the thick brush that marked the edge of the trees. "So what do you think?"

Diana gasped, her aching leg muscles and sore feet forgotten as she gazed at the view. The cove was much smaller than the others they'd seen on their trek around the island, but the water, sheltered by the rocky arms of land that extended out on each side, gleamed like a rare jewel. A dozen shades of blue and green shimmered just beyond the pristine white sand, while a soft breeze stirred the blossoms on the hibiscus bushes that gave the cove its name. Enchantment surrounded them.

"Oh, Trevor, it . . . Now I know what people mean when they say that something takes their breath away."

"I found it last summer when I was out fishing. There isn't a regular path and the road doesn't come anywhere close, so . . ." Trevor seemed to hesitate for a moment, then added, "I thought you'd like it."

Diana turned from the view to meet his gaze. His expression was oddly solemn, yet the moment their eyes met, she felt a surge of warmth flowing between them as though they were about to share something very special. As perhaps they were, she conceded, caught up in the magic. "I'm so glad you brought me here, I love it."

"Then you do agree it's worth hiking the extra mile?" He broke the mesmerizing moment by turning away, his tone now teasing as he headed across the sand toward the water.

Diana swallowed a sigh, wishing again that he wasn't giving her such mixed signals. One minute she'd be feeling close to him, as if they were really becoming friends; then, just as quickly, he'd be pulling away, as though he felt he had to keep his distance. If he'd been anyone but Trevor Sinclair, she might have suspected that he was shy.

Unable to think of anything that would bring back the moment of special closeness, she simply kicked off her sandals and helped him spread the bright island-print tablecloth on the sand, then sank down beside the open hamper. Maybe food would get her brain started again. If she was going to get to know the real Trevor Sinclair before she talked to him about Crystal, she'd have to get busy. They'd done a lot of laughing and talking on their tour, but none of it had touched on their personal lives or feelings.

What really surprised her was that he hadn't asked her any more questions about her reasons for coming to Bellington Cay. He had to be curious. It was un-doubtedly just a matter of time until he started asking questions. Her stomach knotted.

When in doubt, take the initiative; that had been Ken's favorite maxim and, in this case, she had a feel-ing it might be the right one to follow. The trouble was she had no idea how to start. She poured lemonade while Trevor heaped food on two plates, then passed one to her.

Diana tasted the conch salad, then forced her brain into action, sure that if she didn't begin now, she never would. "Is this why you moved to Bellington Cay, Trevor? I mean, because you love the beach and the slower pace of living on an island?"

She sensed his change of mood immediately, though he continued to eat and didn't even look in her direc-tion. Maybe that was why she knew she'd touched a nerve—he'd been directing his sexy pirate grin at her all day.

"I came here because it was one of the few proper-ties I owned that I'd never shared with my wife." He seemed fascinated by the pattern of food on his plate, though he was now merely moving the salad around with his fork.

"Your wife?" Diana caught her breath, totally shocked, though she wasn't sure why she should be.

Still, it seemed strange that he hadn't mentioned having a wife before this. And, for that matter, if he did have a wife, what was he doing inviting a woman to share his house? A flash of anger blazed, then died away as she recognized the pain in his eyes.

"Amanda died almost a year ago." His tone was oddly devoid of emotion.

"I'm sorry, I didn't mean . . ." She let it trail off, wanting to bring the light back into his eyes but not sure what to say. Words were so inadequate. "I had no idea . . ."

"There's no reason why you should know." He met her gaze and his grin returned, though the shadows still lurked in his eyes. "I came here thinking that it would be easier to get over losing her in a place we'd never shared, but I was wrong. I'm finally beginning to realize that running away never works."

For a moment her compassion held steady, then memories of the way he'd deserted Eileen and Crystal surfaced and her heart hardened against his suffering. He hadn't been worried about Eileen's hurt eighteen years ago and he certainly had run out on Crystal when he stopped sending her support checks two years ago.

"Is something wrong, Diana?" Trevor's frown told her that her emotions must have been showing in her face.

For a moment she considered making up another story, something that would enable her to change the subject, but deep down, she knew she couldn't go on pretending she was just a casual visitor to his island and his home. She'd never been good at playing games with the truth and after the time she'd spent with Trevor, she didn't feel right continuing the lie. It was time he knew who she was and why she was here.

She took a deep breath and plunged in, hoping that she hadn't waited too long already. "I agree that running away just makes things worse, and for that reason, I think perhaps it's time I told you why I'm here."

She looked almost frightened, Trevor realized, but there was also a determination about her expression that fascinated him. His laughing guest had disappeared, but the woman before him was no less interesting. "I was hoping you'd decide to trust me."

"Trust you?" That rankled, even though logic told her it was a completely normal response since he didn't know who she was. She swallowed a bitter retort about what had happened to Eileen, focusing on Crystal's needs, not her own sense of justice. "Yes, I guess that is what I'll have to do."

His frown told her that her words had confused him, but he said nothing. For a heartbeat, she lost herself in the depths of his eyes, then she resolutely looked away, unnerved by the attraction she felt. Last night's fantasy pirate and this morning's friendly tour guide were just figments of her imagination; this man was the enemy, the monster who'd hurt the people she loved.

But where to begin? With the basics seemed the best idea. "First of all, my name is Diana Johnson Foster. I'm divorced." She waited, but his expression didn't change. Clearly, her name meant nothing to him, which wasn't surprising, considering the years and the fact that they'd never met. She swallowed hard, then continued. "Eileen Johnson was my sister."

"Eileen . . . ?" For a moment he just looked confused, then his eyes brightened. "Eileen Johnson, that takes me back. You're her little sister? The one she called DeeDee? That must be why you looked so familiar. I spent half the night trying to figure out where I could have seen you and . . ." He let it trail off, his frown returning. "Did Eileen ask you to look me up or something?"

"Not exactly." Diana hesitated, suddenly not sure where to go from here. She'd expected him to look guilty, not curious. "My sister died nearly six years ago."

"Oh, I'm sorry. I had no idea. I . . ."

For a moment, she wanted to hit him, to make him hurt the way she and Crystal and Mom had hurt when Eileen died, but her flash of hate turned into confusion as he continued to gaze at her expectantly. Why wasn't he asking about Crystal now that he knew Eileen was dead?

Trevor watched the flickering emotions as they passed over Diana's expressive features, trying to make sense of them but failing miserably. She looked angry, but he could see no reason why she should be. Eileen had walked out of his life eighteen years ago. Surely he could be excused for not remembering her immediately. Not that he wasn't sorry about Eileen, but . . .

Since she didn't seem willing to continue, he decided to force the issue. "Does my having known your sister have something to do with your coming here, Diana?"

His calmness was too much. Did the man have no feelings? "Something to do with it? It has everything to do with it! I'm here to talk to you about your daughter."

"My what?"

"Your daughter, Crystal Johnson. The one you so conveniently forgot a couple of years ago." Diana set her glass and plate on the cloth; her hands were shaking so much now, she was afraid she'd drop the dishes if she didn't put them down. Besides, even looking at the food made her slightly nauseous.

"I don't know what you're talking about." His expression changed from confused to cold and hard. "This makes no sense at all."

"You're damned right it doesn't." Anger and doubt warred inside her. Could anyone be so utterly callous? She didn't want to believe that the man who'd been so kind and friendly to her could be so devoid of ethics that he'd deny his own child; yet she knew he had once already—eighteen years ago. "As far as I can see, where Crystal is concerned, nothing you've ever done has made any sense."

His gaze had the hard edge of green ice as it lanced into her. "If you've come up with some crazy scheme to claim that I fathered a child by Eileen, you can forget it. I have no children." Contempt twisted his once appealing mouth.

The ugliness of his accusation and the fact that he would suspect her of such a horrible thing hurt terribly. She got to her feet, clenching her shaking hands into fists, fighting the desire to attack him. The hell she'd gone through at Ken's hands had taught her self-control and now she drew on all her reserves, taking a deep breath before she tried to speak.

"There's no point in continuing your denial, Trevor. Eileen is dead and I made no promises. Whether you care about Crystal or not, she is your child and she needs your continued support. When you stopped the payments two years ago . . ."

"When I what? What payments? What promises? I have no idea what you're talking about." Trevor was on his feet, too, facing her across the width of the tablecloth.

Diana met his gaze, searching his face for some sign that he was lying, that he was trying to deny his own child, but she could find nothing in his face but confusion, doubt, and a touch of anger. The knot in her stomach tightened. Never in her wildest nightmares had she pictured this kind of response.

Trevor turned away, fighting a sudden surge of hope. He and Amanda had wanted children, had even considered adopting when she'd been unable to conceive; but then she'd gotten sick and their time for dreams had run out. He pushed away his pain, then turned back to Diana.

Could she be conning him? Were her arrival and helplessness just a scheme to get money from him? He looked into her eyes and saw his own misery and confusion mirrored. His gut told him she couldn't be faking all the emotions that were reflected in her expression.

Crazy or not, she obviously believed what she was saying; so the next question was, who'd told her all this stuff? His anger faded as he realized the obvious answer.

"Did Eileen tell you we'd had a child together?"

Diana nodded. "She brought Crystal home to Pleasant Valley when she was just a few weeks old. Until then, we hadn't even known that she was pregnant." Diana swallowed hard, remembering all the anger and confusion that had filled the house after Eileen's return. It had been a bad time for all of them, all except Crystal. She'd been a sweet and happy infant, totally oblivious to the chaos created by her birth.

"Because Eileen and I had lived together for a while, you believed that the child was mine." Trevor swallowed a sigh, not surprised but saddened to have solved the problem so easily. "Well, I can assure you that if Eileen had been carrying my child, she never would have left college for New York that way. She must have met someone at the modeling agency and . . ."

"What?" Diana's shocked expression told him that she had no idea what he was talking about.

"The agency that recruited her out of school. That was why she left me. I tried to talk her into waiting at least until after the school year ended, but she had stars in her eyes and nothing could keep her in college. She was so sure she was going to be a cover girl and she certainly was pretty enough. I always expected to see her smiling from the front of some magazine, but I guess . . ." He let it trail off, aware that Diana's eyes were blazing again.

"I don't know what you're talking about, Trevor, but I do know that you supported Crystal for the first fifteen years of her life, so don't bother making up any more stories. I've seen the statements. The records are all at the Pleasant Valley First National if you want to see them. And I have our records showing exactly where all of the money went. I can assure you every cent was spent on Crystal."

His confidence began to ebb. She seemed so sure. A flicker of hope flared in the darkness of his confusion. He fought it, not wanting to believe; to have a child would open up so many possibilities. He shook his head, unable to believe that Eileen wouldn't have told him.

Not that he'd thought of Eileen in years. She'd always seemed like a fantasy, a sweet, romantic girl who'd shared his life so briefly, then disappeared without a trace. Once Amanda had come along, he'd discovered true love and nothing else had mattered.

"Are you sure they were my checks?" he asked, reaching out for reality before he succumbed to his longing to believe what Diana was telling him.

A flicker of uncertainty showed in her face, but she didn't back away from the question. "I don't know who signed them, but they were all issued by Sinclair, Inc., and they were all written to the Crystal Johnson Trust. I don't see how you can pretend that you've never heard of her."

"Sinclair, Inc." Trevor sat down abruptly, his knees suddenly refusing to support him. "Dear God, if you're telling the truth . . ." He couldn't go on.

"What do you mean, if I'm telling the truth? I can call the bank and have photocopies sent out if you want, but why should I?" Anger made her voice rough. "If you want proof, I can give it to you a lot easier than that." Diana sank down, too, and he watched as she took her wallet out of her waist pack and opened it to some snapshots. She held it out to him without a word.

Heart pounding, Trevor took the wallet and looked down the long tunnel into his own past. For a moment he thought he was looking at Eileen——the cloud of pale golden hair and elfin grin were hers, but the eyes . . . He tried to swallow, but his throat didn't work and he nearly choked. The defiant green- and gold-flecked hazel eyes that stared back at him could have been his own.

"Are you still going to deny that you have a daughter?" Diana expected to feel triumph, but Trevor's stunned expression made it clear that he really hadn't known about Crystal. She watched as he looked through the other snapshots, saw the flash of pain in his eyes as he studied the one of Eileen and baby Crystal. He looked so vulnerable, almost as though he was afraid to trust the evidence before his eyes. The last of her anger and resentment drained away, replaced by compassion and a need to know how this could have happened.

"What happened, Trevor? Why didn't you know about the baby?" She hesitated, then added, "I don't understand how you could have been paying for Crystal's care all these years and not realize . . ."

It seemed an eternity before Trevor finally lifted his gaze from the pictures, and when he did, he looked every one of his thirty-eight years. "I had nothing whatsoever to do with sending those checks, Diana. Sinclair, Inc., is my father's company, not mine. I've never had any part in running it. After I graduated from college, Harlan Cole, my wife Amanda, and I built our own company together—ATS Industries."

"Are you saying that your father was the one who supported Crystal all those years?" Diana was torn between relief at this proof that Trevor wasn't the monster she'd believed him to be and a cynical skepticism that warned her not to be so eager to exonerate him.

"So it would seem." His eyes grew cold and his lips became a thin, pale line of anger. "And the bastard never bothered to mention it to me." His hands had become fists, the knuckles white against his tan.

"You really never knew?" Why did she want so much to believe him?

"If I'd known, I would never have just sent money, Diana. This is my *daughter*. . . ." His voice broke and it was several minutes before he regained control of himself. "When did you say the money stopped arriving?"

"About two years ago." Diana frowned. That seemed like an odd question. Could he still doubt his paternity?

"That's when Dad had his stroke. Felice, that's his second wife, took over control of the company at that time. She's probably the one who stopped the payments. And, of course, she wouldn't have any reason to tell me." His expression changed and this time his anger blazed in her direction. "But why didn't you or your mother or even Crystal? Why didn't anyone tell me?"

"You didn't want to know. That was the agreement. In return for support, Eileen agreed never to make any claim on you where your child was concerned." The answer was so familiar to her, the words were out before she realized that they couldn't be true.

"Who told you that?" The chill in his eyes was like a cold mist on her skin.

"Eileen. When she came home with the baby, she told us that she'd made the promise. She was so hurt and angry. Mom wanted her to say she'd been married to you, but Eileen refused. She said you'd given up all claim to Crystal, that she'd never have your name. You broke her heart."

"That's a lie."

"What?" The sharpness of his tone scraped over her already raw nerves. "How dare you . . ."

Trevor lifted a hand, stopping her angry words. "I don't know what happened, Diana. I told you, Eileen left me. She went off to New York to accept a job with a modeling agency. She was supposed to call me so I could join her after finals, but she never did. Then Dad came up with an offer of a trip to Europe and . . ." He sighed. "I tried calling the agency, but I never could catch her, so, well, I figured she'd made her choice and her career was more important to her than I was.''

"And Eileen ended up having her baby all alone somewhere.'' Diana shook her head, trying hard to remember everything that had happened seventeen years ago. She'd been a rather naive twelve when Eileen came home, so Mom had done her best to shut her out of most of the discussions she and Eileen had; but Diana had managed to overhear some of them. "I still don't understand. Eileen never mentioned your father; she told us that you didn't want Crystal. I'm sure she thought the checks were coming from you. She told us often enough that you promised support only as long as she never tried to contact you.''

"That's just not true. My father must have told her that. If I had known . . . I would never have let my child grow up without knowing me. She could have lived with us, had the very best of everything. We could have . . .'' He let it trail off, forcing the shadows of the past from his mind. "But none of that matters now. Tell me about Crystal. I want to know everything about my daughter. Where is she? What's happened that made you come here to see me? She's not ill or in some kind of trouble?''

There was no mistaking the honest hunger in his face; it reached out to her, banishing the last of her doubts about him. She settled herself more comfortably on the sand and began describing Crystal's life—her years growing up in Pleasant Valley, Diana's own closeness to her niece, the emerging musical talent that had outgrown the teachers available in such a small town.

"She's in her final year at Cliffton School for Girls now. That's the boarding school where I was working. They have a very fine music program there, which is why I was able to arrange for Crystal to audition for entrance to the Wilding School of Music last spring. At the time, of course, I had no idea that there wouldn't be enough money for her tuition.''

Trevor's rapt expression suddenly congealed. "That's why you came? For the money?"

His tone bothered her, but Diana continued, not sure why he suddenly seemed so angry. Surely he couldn't resent his daughter's ambitions. "Crystal is a marvelous pianist, but she hasn't much chance of ever reaching the concert stage without further training. With Mom's illness and my losing my position at Cliffton . . ." Diana let it trail off, aware that his expression had grown even darker. "I'd be happy to sign a note for the money. It might take me a while to pay it all back, but I will find another position and once Mom sells the shop . . ."

"You just expect me to hand over a check?" His eyes blazed with outrage.

Diana swallowed hard, not sure what she'd done to infuriate him. "I didn't . . . Don't you want your daughter to have the chance she deserves?"

"I want my daughter, damn it! Haven't you people robbed me of enough of her life? I'm not going to just pay for things, Diana. You can't keep shutting me out; I'm going to be a part of Crystal's life from now on."

She opened her mouth to reply, but no words came. A chill slithered over her skin as she realized that she should have expected this. The moment she'd accepted the fact that Trevor didn't know about Crystal, everything had changed and now she had no idea what to do or say to defuse the situation—if it could be defused now that Trevor knew he had a daughter.

"I'm sorry, Trevor," she began, choosing her words with care. "I didn't even think . . . I mean, when I decided to come here, all I was concerned about was Crystal and what she needs. Please forgive me for being insensitive, but you have to remember, I've always believed that you didn't care about Crystal."

For a moment, his temper continued to simmer, then he forced back the tide of anger. This wasn't Diana's doing; she'd come here because she obviously loved

Crystal—loved his daughter—enough to face a man she'd expected to hate in order to make Crystal's dreams a reality. It wasn't her fault—she'd been lied to by an expert.

He forced a grin that felt a little tight. "I realize none of this is your fault. And it's not mine either. If my father wasn't already in a wheelchair, I'd happily fly to Denver and put him in one for this. He's the one who robbed both Crystal and me."

"How could he do such a thing?" She closed her eyes, lost for a moment in memories of her own loving father.

"He probably told himself he was just protecting me. A forced marriage would have thrown his timetable off. He knew that Eileen had left me, so he undoubtedly figured money was the perfect solution. What I can't understand is why he never told me, not even after I married Amanda."

Diana observed the cold anger that had etched his face, and she shivered in spite of the warm afternoon sun. She had a strong hunch that his father's only thought had been to avoid that implacable fury and she hated the man because he hadn't cared that he'd cheated everyone involved. "You aren't the only one he robbed. Eileen's life was scarred, too."

Trevor sighed, then picked up his discarded plate of food. "He's going to have some explaining to do when I call him after we get back to the house. Meantime, we might as well finish our picnic."

Diana picked up her own plate, trying to match his calm, but her throat was already closing, letting her know she'd never be able to swallow a morsel. What had she done? Suddenly, all the implications of Trevor's interest in his daughter filled her mind. She'd come here hoping to be able to protect Crystal from an uncaring father; but now it appeared she might have an even more difficult problem, that of protecting her from a father she claimed she didn't even want to know.

"So why don't you tell me more about Crystal? I want to know everything about her."

"That's a tall order." Her voice sounded scratchy, no doubt from the lump in her throat. "I don't know where to begin."

"Well, where is the school? The one Crystal is attending." His question surprised her.

"It's in Sutton Falls, Illinois. That's a small town not too far from Chicago. Why?"

"I'm going there as soon as I can get on a plane."

"You can't!" She gasped the words without thinking.

Trevor stiffened, the glow of excitement fading from his eyes. "And why not? I've already missed seventeen years of my daughter's life, I'm not going to miss another minute."

The determination in his face fueled her anxiety. She couldn't stop him, yet she had to do something or this could become a terrible mess. She took a deep breath, praying for the right words. "I know how desperately you must want to meet her, but, Trevor, you can't just fly up there and introduce yourself. She's grown up believing that you never wanted her. I'm afraid she's going to have a hard time accepting the truth."

"All the more reason she has to be told. The sooner the better." Impatience fueled his determination. He'd never allowed anyone else to direct his life and he wasn't about to start now. Once she knew the truth, Crystal would accept him. Hell, she needed him. Besides, she was his daughter—that had to mean something.

"I agree that she has to be told the truth. The question is how and by whom. It's going to be a shock and I don't want it to upset her so much that she does something foolish."

The worry he could read in Diana's eyes dissolved his fantasy about holding Crystal in his arms while she cried with joy at their meeting. "What could she do?"

Diana sighed. "She's seventeen, Trevor. I've been teaching teenagers since I graduated from college and

I wouldn't even venture a guess. The point is, she's tied up with school until the Thanksgiving vacation. That starts next week. I just think it might be better for you both if you wait until then to meet.''

"You expect me to wait another week?''

She could see the impatience in his face, sense his anxiety, yet she had to buy time—time to decide how best to protect Crystal and maybe herself. "That's a week when she'll be busy completing assignments and taking tests. She needs to have her mind on her studies. This opportunity at Wilding could be lost if her grades suddenly nosedive.''

Was she stalling? Trevor studied Diana's face closely, wanting to believe that she was just putting him off because she didn't want him to meet Crystal; but he found nothing in her eyes to substantiate that theory. His initial blaze of enthusiasm began to subside. He definitely didn't want to start out on the wrong foot with his daughter, but could he trust Diana's instincts? Did he have a choice?

Another question intruded. "Does she know you're here? That you came to see me?''

Diana nodded, wondering where this might be leading. She sensed that she'd shaken his initial resolve to rush right to Crystal, but she also suspected that he'd merely been momentarily diverted. Though she'd known him less than twenty-four hours, she already suspected that Trevor Sinclair was a man determined to have his own way.

"So she knows you came to ask me for money?''

"I had to tell her that the tuition money wasn't in her account.'' At least, she'd thought she had to at the time. Right now, she rather wished she'd kept her mouth shut.

"So Crystal will be expecting to hear from you soon.'' He looked pleased at the idea. "About your success or failure.''

"I expect so.'' It wasn't exactly a phone call she

was looking forward to making, especially now. "She has a lot of dreams, Trevor, and most of them revolve around her music."

And not her father, he realized. But that could be changed. He would change it, he decided, a plan beginning to form in his mind. "I suppose you could be right about waiting for our meeting, but only until next week. I want Crystal to come here for the Thanksgiving vacation. That should give us a good chance to get acquainted."

"What?"

"I want you to call her today and tell her about the lies, then explain to her that the three of us will be spending the holiday here. That will give us nearly a week to make our plans and she'll have time to get used to the idea of having a real father, so everything should be fine." He gave her what he hoped was a confident smile. "What do you think?"

A part of her mind screamed protests, but the vulnerability and longing in his eyes forced her to ignore everything but his need. He deserved a chance and she had no right to try to stop him. She swallowed hard. "I'll call her tonight."

His grin was her reward, but it didn't change her feeling that, by following her heart, she'd just made a decision that would change all their lives forever. She only hoped she wouldn't live to regret it.

FOUR

The rest of the afternoon passed much too quickly for Diana, mostly because she kept thinking about her promise to call Crystal. What the devil was she going to tell her? How could she make a seventeen-year-old understand what she was still having a hard time accepting?

Not that she doubted Trevor's story—she'd heard more than enough of his furious accusations when he'd called his father after they got back from their picnic. But she'd met Trevor, spent time with him, come to like him even before . . .

Diana sighed and turned over to give the setting sun a chance to warm her back. It was time to go in, but once she did, she knew that Trevor would start watching her expectantly again. Not that she blamed him for being eager to have Crystal know that he cared; it was just that she couldn't shake the feeling that Crystal was going to be upset by the news.

Trevor stood by the kitchen window, watching Diana as she lay on the beach. How long was she planning to stay out there? Another hour and she'd be working on a moontan. His impatience crackled through him like static electricity. She was stalling. But why? He'd told her what his father had said. Surely she couldn't have any doubts about his feelings, his need to meet this miracle child he'd suddenly discovered.

"What time will you be wanting dinner tonight, Trevor?" Louise broke into his dark thoughts.

"Let me check with Diana." He jumped at the opportunity to lure her inside to where the telephone waited.

Forty-five minutes later, Diana gave her hair a final pat, smoothed the full skirt of her coral and white cotton dress, then met her own gaze in the mirror. It was time; if she stalled any longer, Crystal would have left for the dining room and she might not return to her room until time for lights out. A tempting scenario, but one that would only prolong her own tension.

Feeling like a condemned criminal on her last walk, she headed for the room next to hers, the one Trevor had told her was his office. He'd suggested that she use the phone there, so she'd have privacy for her call. She spoke with the overseas operator, then leaned back in the chair and closed her eyes as she waited for the call to go through. What was she going to say?

A rush of love swept over her as she heard Crystal's familiar voice. She managed a smile as she told her that she was calling from Trevor Sinclair's home on Bellington Cay. It was good news she had for her, wasn't it? All she needed to do was find the right words . . .

Anxiety and impatience mingled in Crystal's voice as she interrupted, "Did you ask him yet, Diana? Will he pay my tuition so I can go to Wilding?"

"We've been talking about it, honey, but there's something more important that you need to know. Something that I just found out today." Diana took a deep breath and, resigned to never finding the perfect way to tell Crystal, just let the words spill out, stating the truth that she'd learned. When she finally ran out of breath, the silence from the other end was deafening.

Aware that Crystal would undoubtedly have a little

trouble digesting so much new information, she tried to be patient; but after what seemed an eternity, she couldn't help wondering if something had happened to the connection. "Crystal, are you still there? Are you all right?"

"You believe him? I mean, he really didn't know about me?" Crystal's voice sounded very young and unsure.

Sympathy swept through her. She'd had trouble accepting the truth, so why should she expect Crystal to find it easy? "He's a nice man, honey, really. I'm sure if he'd known . . ." She hesitated, then edited the truth slightly, sure that Crystal shouldn't hear the details of her grandfather's cruel duplicity just yet. "His father probably thought Trevor was too young to be tied down to a wife and child, so he must have lied to your mother, pretended that he was speaking for Trevor when he made her promise never to contact him."

"So what does he want from me?" The lack of feeling in Crystal's voice made Diana shiver. She'd expected tears or joy or wonder, but not cynicism.

"He wants to meet you. He was ready to fly out tomorrow, but I convinced him that he should wait until vacation. I know how busy you are now." She paused, hoping for a response, but her usually talkative niece had suddenly become very taciturn. "Anyway, he wants you to fly out here for Thanksgiving vacation."

"No."

"What?" Diana's chill deepened. This was definitely not going as she'd expected.

"I don't want to meet him. He can keep his old money. I'll get a scholarship or . . ." Her anger came through loud and clear.

Sensing that it was fear that fueled Crystal's temper, Diana swallowed her own angry words. This was no time for an ultimatum. "Trevor's invitation has nothing to do with money, Crystal. He's your father. He wants to see you, get to know you, help you plan your future.''

"Do you want me to come?" Doubt had crept into her voice.

"Of course. That's why I agreed to stay here and help him get ready for your visit."

"You're going to be there? You won't leave?" The relief in Crystal's voice explained her initial refusal.

"Didn't I tell you that?" Diana cursed her own scattered thoughts. "I would never ask you to fly down here to spend time alone with a stranger. I'll be here the whole time, I promise." She waited, hoping for enthusiasm, but Crystal didn't respond. "Wouldn't you like to spend your vacation on the beach? I was out sunning all afternoon and it was heavenly."

"He really just wants to talk to me?"

Diana heaved a sigh of relief as she sensed the change in Crystal's attitude. So what if it took the promise of a sunny beach, all that mattered was that Crystal come to Bellington Cay. After that it was up to Trevor. "Don't you want to get to know your father?"

"I guess it might be okay." Not exactly a ringing endorsement, but Diana was grateful for any sign of progress. It was, she knew, going to take a great deal of time and patience—on everyone's part.

Once the arrangements were made, she replaced the receiver and leaned back, weak with relief at having accomplished her mission. After several restful moments, she looked around, her curiosity about the man whose life she'd just changed suddenly reviving. What she saw put a damper on her enthusiasm.

The room was a shrine, there was no other word for it. Framed photographs were everywhere and the subject was the same in all of them—girl or woman, alone or with friends, Amanda Sinclair looked out from each frame. If he'd come to the island hoping to forget the pain of her death, Trevor had picked an odd way to go about it.

Diana picked up the handsome color portrait that stood on the corner of Trevor's desk. His wife had been beautiful, there was no question about that. And brainy, too, considering what he'd told her about the way they'd built up the business together. A paragon, no doubt; the perfect woman for him.

She hated herself for the resentment she felt, knowing that it was misplaced. According to Trevor, he'd met Amanda after Eileen disappeared from his life, so there was no way she could be blamed for the unhappiness of Eileen's life. Yet she couldn't shake the feeling that all of this should have been Eileen's and Crystal's. Or was she wishing it were hers?

Stunned by the implications of her own thoughts, Diana got to her feet. What was wrong with her? She'd barely escaped a bad marriage six months ago; how could she even entertain romantic thoughts about a man? She cast a last glance over her shoulder, meeting the friendly gaze of the woman in the portrait, then turned out the light and fled down the staircase as though Amanda was in pursuit.

Trevor rose from where he'd been sitting on one of the couches, his worried expression making her ashamed of the extra time she'd kept him waiting. "Is she coming?"

She nodded, suddenly finding the lump in her throat too large to swallow. His longing was so obvious, his concern plain in his eyes; she ached with regret, thinking that he would have made a wonderfully caring father during all the difficult times that Crystal had been through. Years that his father's selfishness had stolen from them.

"When . . . ?"

"She'll let us know for sure as soon as she makes her reservations. It depends on how soon she can get a flight after her last test, but she should be here sometime next Wednesday."

His grin split the darkness of his beard and joy blazed

in golden highlights in the depths of his eyes. "How did she sound?" He looked like a little boy eagerly anticipating a visit from Santa.

Only it wasn't going to be all that easy or pleasant, Diana reminded herself. "Shocked, a little frightened, curious." She hated turning out the light in his eyes, but she sensed that he needed to be prepared for the reality of what lay ahead. Crystal had lived with hate and anger for seventeen years; it might take more than four days of sun and sand with Trevor to erase the damage the lies had done.

"But not enthusiastic." It wasn't a question.

"It's going to take her some time, Trevor. You've been the enemy for her entire life. The man who never wanted to know her. The man who broke her mother's heart."

"But you told her that it was all lies; that none of it was my fault." His protest was so softly spoken she felt rather than heard the pain that fueled it.

"I still have flashes of anger at you and I know you aren't guilty of anything. And I liked you even before I learned the truth. She has no frame of reference, just my explanation and she's too old to accept any adult opinion without questioning it." She phrased it as kindly as she could as she sat down beside him on the couch.

"It's not going to be easy, is it?" His expression told her that she'd gotten her point across.

"At least she's coming and once she gets to know you . . ." It took all her self-control not to reach out to him, to offer him a comforting touch. But she didn't dare, not when she was so unsure of her own feelings. Or when she remembered the picture-haunted office where she'd made the call.

They sat in a rather uneasy silence until Louise came in to tell them that dinner was ready. Diana swallowed hard as she got to her feet, suddenly aware that Louise would be leaving as soon as they sat down to eat . . . and she would once again be alone here with Trevor.

"You'll help me, won't you? I mean, I'm not sure how to talk to a teenager. If she were still a little girl, I could buy her toys and . . . But she's only a couple of years younger now than her mother was when we were together." He shook his head as he pulled out one of the handsome dining room chairs for her. "Lord, how can that be?"

Sensing a surprising undercurrent of panic in Trevor's voice, Diana forced away her own fears and doubts, well aware that he needed reassurance now. "Don't think about the wasted years," she counseled. "Think of what you can still share. You can get to know her, have a real part in her life now; that's what's important. Given a little time . . ."

Trevor settled himself at the head of the table, confidence once again obvious in his expression. "You're right. Beginnings are always tough, but she'll be here and once she finds out how much I want to help her and guide her and love her, she'll have to trust and believe in me. She'll know how important having a father can be."

"Right." She did her best to echo his enthusiasm, but a tiny chill traced down her spine even as she agreed. Once Crystal was comfortable with her father, would she still need Diana's love and guidance?

"Tell me more about her. What exactly is she studying? How are her grades? What subjects does she like best?" His questions forced her mind back from her fears.

Trevor watched Diana's face as she talked about Crystal, reveling equally in the joy of learning about his daughter and the pleasure of just watching Diana. Her eyes glowed when she spoke about her niece, and the depth of her love for Crystal was obvious in every tale she told him. In fact . . . He frowned, suddenly realizing what was wrong with her stories.

"Where was Eileen during this time?" he asked, interrupting her story about Crystal's first piano recital.

Diana's expression changed at once, the animation draining from her face. "I'm not sure. She . . . she never could find a job she liked in Pleasant Valley, so she was gone quite often while Crystal was growing up. She knew Mom and I would take care of Crystal and she liked earning her own way. She hated the idea of ever being dependent on your . . . your father's handouts."

He swallowed a sigh, not missing the undercurrent of anger in Diana's voice—or the defensiveness. He felt a pang of pity for Eileen, remembering how bright and beautiful she'd been, like a butterfly drifting through his life, bringing laughter and joy, then moving on without a trace. Or so he'd thought until he'd seen the photo of Crystal. "Was she still modeling?"

Diana's gaze evaded his. "I really don't know. Probably. She never talked much about what she did while she was gone; but she always came home happy, loaded down with presents for all of us. I kept hoping that she'd stay that way, but after a while the shadows would start to grow in her eyes and I knew that she'd be leaving again."

"And what about Crystal, didn't her mother's absences bother her?"

Diana stiffened and her eyes blazed as she met his gaze. "She knew her mother loved her. Besides, she had Mom and me, so she didn't need anyone else."

"Like a father?" The words were out before he could stop them and he knew at once that he'd made a mistake. Diana's words about forgetting the past and concentrating on the future suddenly made a lot more sense. The past appeared to be a mine field and he was already blundering into trouble. He forced his own feelings aside and concentrated on Diana, hoping he could salvage the moment. "I'm sorry, I didn't mean to question Eileen's mothering, Diana. I just wondered how Crystal felt. If she could forgive her mother's absences, perhaps she'll be more understanding about my seeming neglect.''

Diana studied him, fighting her own anger, suddenly remembering all the times that Crystal had cried in her arms because she missed her mother. Times she had no intention of mentioning to Trevor. There was no way she'd let him use Eileen's occasional neglect to win his way into Crystal's life.

''We got along fine. Crystal just had three mothers instead of one. She missed Eileen, but she knew she'd come back.'' She tried to ignore the hurt in his gaze, but she couldn't. This was not his fault. ''And she'll learn to accept the fact that you never knew about her and she'll understand that you were hurt by your father's lies, too. You'll just have to be patient.''

''We all will.'' He picked up her hand, his fingers warm and strong as they closed over hers. ''We'll help each other.''

A shiver that had nothing to do with the past or Crystal moved over her skin and she couldn't keep her own fingers from twining through his. The man was too appealing to be for real, she told herself; but she had a hunch her better sense wasn't paying attention, not while she was busy losing herself in the warmth of his gaze.

It was just chemistry, she was convinced as she forced her attention back to her food. She hadn't been this close to a really interesting man since before Ken Foster came to Cliffton, so it wasn't surprising that she was a little vulnerable. And being alone with him in an island paradise didn't help her self-control. She'd just have to keep reminding herself that he was Crystal's father and not a potential . . . She refused to even think the word ''lover.''

''What would you like to do after dinner?'' Trevor asked, interrupting her unnerving thoughts.

''I . . . ah . . . hadn't really thought . . .'' Her brain

seemed to be stuck in slow gear. "What are my options?"

"Well, since this is Friday, both the resorts will have bands for dancing. There's also the movie theater, which is open on weekends. And the Jolly Roger will be in full swing." His soft chuckle lifted her pulse rate. "That's about the extent of the nightlife on the island, unless you're into moonlight walks along the beach."

That suggestion warmed her even more than the touch of his fingers, proof positive that she shouldn't go. Unfortunately, she had no enthusiasm for dancing and, after last night, no desire to return to the Jolly Roger. Her inner warning voice suggested pleading weariness so she could go to bed and read a good book, but she was in no mood for good advice.

A voice that definitely didn't sound like hers was already saying, "I'd love a walk, especially after all this delicious food. Louise is truly a treasure."

"That's what I keep telling her." His sexy gaze seemed to stroke her face, his eyes hypnotic.

Was this what the poor mouse felt when it faced the fearsome beauty of the cobra? But the cobra was cruel and she knew now that Trevor was gentle and kind and . . . and incredibly dangerous to her fragile emotions. The extent of her own weakness where Trevor was concerned startled her back into sanity. What the devil was wrong with her? She'd never been so easily attracted. Guilt and confusion swept through her as she gently freed her fingers and pretended an interest in her coffee.

Trevor watched her, intrigued by the myriad emotions that were obvious in her face. He wasn't sure exactly what Diana was feeling, but he could sure see that she was feeling something. And he liked it. That fact startled him. It seemed like a lifetime since he'd been this interested in anyone else's feelings. Not since Amanda.

For just a heartbeat he felt the sharp spur of guilt, then it faded. Diana wasn't just anyone, she was Crystal's aunt, the woman who'd helped raise his daughter. A feeling of wry humor stole through him. Right, and her relationship to Crystal was exactly why he wanted to take her walking on the beach. His deep interest in Diana had nothing to do with her warmth, her quick mind, her intriguing smile, her long, lovely legs. He hadn't been on the island long enough to believe that!

The silence was beginning to bug Diana. She shifted in her chair and sought a subject that would put them back on a casual-friend basis. "So tell me, what sort of music do they have at the resorts?"

"I'm not sure. I've never spent the holidays here. I just heard Joe mention that one of his cousins would be playing." He grinned at her. "In case you haven't already guessed from talking to Louise, she and Joe are pretty much related to half the population of the island. We can ask her about the bands tomorrow, if you like. Or maybe we could just check them out tomorrow night."

"That might be fun. If you have the time, that is." She tried hard to keep in mind that she wasn't just his guest, that he'd asked her to stay so they could prepare for Crystal's visit.

"I have nothing but time, Diana. I'll enjoy exploring the possibilities." He met her gaze boldly and she felt as though the tropical sun was still beating down on her.

Diana forced her mind away from the delicious quiver of excitement his words sent through her. "We'll have to talk about things to do while Crystal's here, too."

"No reason why she can't go enjoy the music. The resorts cater to all ages, so there will be plenty of other teenagers in attendance, I'm sure. Or there may be other island traditions that we can share with her. That's something else we can ask Louise about. I'm going to have to make a list."

Hearing the enthusiasm and excitement in his voice

made her want to smile, yet another part of her felt more like crying. How could she ever compete with all that Trevor could offer Crystal? And why did she feel as though she might have to?

"So are you ready for our walk?"

Startled, Diana looked down at her plate and realized that she'd finished her dessert without even tasting it. But she wasn't ready, not for being alone with him in the velvet darkness. Yet how could she refuse when she'd already accepted? And when she wanted very much to go? Never had she felt so confused by her own emotions and she hated it. She knew she had to escape his scrutiny, at least until she could regain control of her wayward feelings.

"If we're going to be walking in the sand, I'm going to change into sneakers. I spent enough time emptying sand out of my sandals this afternoon." She rose so quickly, she nearly upset her water glass. "See you in a few minutes."

Trevor frowned as he watched her run up the stairs. What had he done? She'd acted almost frightened. But going for a walk on the beach had been her choice. Could she have changed her mind? But why? Surely she must realize that he would never do anything to . . . Just because he'd been wondering what it would feel like to hold her, to kiss her, didn't mean that he had any intention of taking advantage of their newly formed alliance.

Or maybe it had nothing to do with him. He frowned as he remembered the terse way she'd told him that she was divorced. He'd tried to get her talking about herself a couple of times earlier today, before she'd told him exactly who she was, but she'd always turned his questions away. She'd used humor, but she'd made it clear that she didn't want to discuss her past.

He shook his head, wondering what kind of man would let a woman like Diana get away. A fool, that was sure. Probably some oversexed college jock who couldn't appreciate the depth of her character or who might have been jealous of her relationship with Crystal.

Could that have been it? It irritated him to realize how little he knew about Diana. He got to his feet, suddenly eager for the walk. Tonight he wasn't going to let her dodge his questions. Her past was a part of Crystal's life and he needed to know everything he could about his daughter. And about Diana.

He was waiting at the foot of the stairs. Diana caught her breath as he looked up at her. A pirate with the eyes of a poet and the sex appeal of . . . well, she wasn't about to get into that again. She'd just spent the last ten minutes convincing herself that her attraction to him was the result of frustration and normal hormones. It didn't help to realize that, if this was normal, she was in trouble. The very thought made her knees wobbly, so she trailed her hand along the banister as she went down.

Trevor's determination to get answers ebbed as he recognized the wariness in Diana's gaze. He might not know what had caused her anxiety, but he sure didn't want to add to it. Besides, he reminded himself, he had plenty of time. Once she knew him better, he was sure she'd be willing to confide in him. And if he was right about her ex-husband being her problem, he'd make sure she knew he would protect her.

The cool, damp air curled around Diana like a drift of soothing mist. Maybe she was just overreacting, worrying needlessly about the chemistry flaring between her and Trevor. Loneliness could be a potent force and he'd obviously come down here to escape his grief, so his interest could just be proof that he was healing.

And her volatile reaction to him? Was it real or just a way to distract herself from the pain of her failed marriage? She knew now that she'd never loved Ken, but that hadn't lessened the pain of having made such a mess of her life. Failure hurt and so did the realization that she'd been a fool.

"Diana, are you all right?" Trevor's voice was soft, but she could hear the concern and realized that her feet had been racing as fast as her thoughts.

"I'm fine, thank you. Just enjoying the night." The lie came easily but left a bad taste as she forced herself to stop and look around. "It really is very beautiful out here."

"Yes, it is." He was looking down at her, his gaze like a caress as it moved over her face. Her heart slowed, then leaped to high speed as he reached out and gently smoothed back a tendril of hair that the breeze was teasing.

A shiver chased down her spine, then changed to heat that pooled deep inside her, before expanding through her entire body. His fingers were so warm and so tender, like his gaze and his sexy mouth . . . She fought back an almost irresistible urge to lick her suddenly dry lips. This was total madness.

Trevor pulled his hand back, shocked at the electricity that seemed to flare from a single touch. When she looked up at him like that, he found it hard to think of anything beyond her striking beauty and the vulnerability he could see in her eyes. Her lips were parted, an invitation that he . . . had damned well better resist!

Trevor forced his gaze away from her tempting mouth and focused on the restless waves that washed the beach. Crystal, he had to think about his daughter now, not Diana. He couldn't risk losing them both by acting like a love-starved teenager. This sudden longing was just the result of his long period without a woman.

He took a deep breath and forced his brain into a less incendiary line of thought. "So, do you miss teaching at Crystal's school?"

Diana stiffened, the illusion of romance destroyed by his question. "I definitely miss teaching and being near Crystal, but the atmosphere at Cliffton was rather restrictive. And, of course, she will be graduating in the spring, so I would probably have been looking for another position, anyway. I mean, I . . .'' She stopped herself, aware that she was babbling, that she really didn't want to explain any further. She didn't mind telling Trevor about Crystal, but her personal life was off-limits to everyone. She hadn't even been able to explain everything to her mother.

Even though he'd moved away from her, Trevor was aware of the change in Diana's mood. Something was bothering her and he was suddenly sure that it had nothing to do with him or Crystal. ''Is that why you quit, because you didn't want to work there after Crystal graduated?''

''I left for a number of reasons. My mother's illness, for one.'' Not to mention the fact that, in a fit of anger over her refusal to reconsider leaving him, Ken Foster had terminated her contract with a totally undeserved attack on her abilities. A vindictive action that still bothered her. Even after she'd realized that she couldn't live with Ken, she hadn't expected him to be so vicious. She sometimes wondered what else he'd done to her reputation after she left the school.

Trevor studied her in the silvery magic of the moonlight. Could her mother's condition be the reason for the sadness in her eyes? He almost hated to ask, since he remembered clearly just how painful it was to discuss the physical condition of someone you loved. ''How serious is her condition?''

''It was more a matter of how serious it could become. She's always worked too long and too hard and the cold, damp winters in Iowa were getting harder and harder for her. This year her sister, my Aunt Betty, invited her to come and stay with her and her husband in Arizona, and since I was home, she could go. The warm, dry climate has done wonders for her.''

''And you stayed behind to run the shop in Pleasant Valley for your mother?'' Trevor tried to put everything she'd told him into order, hoping to make sense of her life, but there seemed to be large empty spaces in the biography. Like where the husband had fit in.

"To run it until the sale went through, which I hope will happen soon. We have a buyer, but financing is a problem these days and . . ." She let it trail off, embarrassed by this turn of the conversation. How could she expect someone like Trevor Sinclair to understand the difficulty of selling a small dress shop or the problems of settling on a down payment that would satisfy Mom's need for income and yet not make the purchase too difficult for the Dahlmer sisters?

Her comments about the business appeared unemotional, Trevor realized, so that couldn't be what was troubling her. It was when she spoke about the school that he sensed her tension. He decided to pursue the subject further. "I imagine Crystal misses having you at Cliffton."

"I don't know about that." Diana forced a smile she was far from feeling. "She used to love having me on staff there, but now she's much too mature to want her aunt hanging around."

Though she'd meant the words to sound humorous, they brought back unpleasant memories. There had been a definite loss of closeness between her and Crystal after she told her niece that she was leaving Ken. For some reason, Crystal actually seemed to resent the fact that she wanted a divorce. It had been a rather tense summer, and once Crystal went back to school in the fall, there'd been few letters or phone calls except those regarding the opening at Wilding. In fact, until the call today, she'd pretty much felt shut out of Crystal's life.

"I suppose you'll be seeking a new position soon?" He was getting nowhere by being subtle, he realized, his frustration growing.

"After the first of the year, if the sale of the shop goes through." Diana swallowed a sigh, feeling her self-doubts more sharply than usual. She'd sent out dozens of letters already and her mailbox had remained ominously empty. "Of course, there aren't likely to be any openings before next fall. It's not exactly a good time to be job hunting."

"Would you like me to make some inquiries? If you could tell me what . . ."

"Oh, no, I'm sorry I even brought it up." Diana shook back her hair and smiled at him. "I'm here to talk about Crystal and put her life in order, not to worry about my future. Something will turn up. It always does. Meanwhile, we have that marvelous dinner to walk off."

"Whatever you say." Trevor caught her hand, lacing his fingers through hers before she could pull away. "Shall we head inland this time? I mean, we did pretty well exploring the beach this afternoon." Her bravado didn't fool him a bit; she was plenty worried about finding a job. He smiled as they headed for the distant band of trees. If she thought she didn't need his help, she was due for a big surprise.

FIVE

Diana felt an odd twinge of disappointment as they drew near the handsome white house. Though they'd talked and laughed like old friends for the past hour, she had the feeling that something unsaid was still simmering between them. Besides, she was much too conscious of the warmth of his arm as it rested lightly on her shoulders, of the beguiling night, the stars that spread above them in a bewildering confusion, the pure moon that cast more than enough light to keep them from stumbling in the rich grass that edged the road.

"Tired?" Trevor asked, the concern in his voice reminding her that she hadn't spoken for several minutes.

"It's so beautiful here. Every once in a while it strikes me and takes my breath away. Living here must be heaven."

Trevor slowed. "Beauty needs to be shared, Diana. I've seen more of it since you've been here than . . ." He let it trail off, not trusting his voice as his throat tightened with remembered grief. When he could speak again, he continued with a lighter note. "I suspect I've enjoyed our exploring as much as you. Even the goats tonight."

Diana giggled. "They weren't very glad to see us, were they?"

"That billy goat was positively homicidal when you tried to pet the little one." Trevor chuckled, his sadness forgotten.

"But you were so brave. I never would have made it through the fence if you hadn't driven him back." Memories of his skirmish with the belligerent goat brought more laughter. Suddenly she felt both young and free. "And you were real quick, too."

"Next time we go hiking in the interior, we'll take some goat repellent with us." Trevor found it hard to keep his face straight.

"Goat repellent? Give me a break, I'm a country girl. If you've ever been real close to a billy goat on a hot afternoon, you know nothing repels goats."

"Well, I'm a city fella, so you'll have to teach me all the tricks of handling the critters." He stopped, tightening his embrace so she had to turn and face him.

Diana caught her breath, her amusement dissolving under the heat of his gaze. She should say something, divert his attention so that they could go inside and . . . And be alone in the empty house. She waited for the shiver of anxiety, but it didn't come. In fact, the quivers that traced through her were more like tiny electric shocks of anticipation.

"Diana." He trailed a finger down the side of her face, then tenderly traced the outline of her lips in a tantalizing caress that heated her blood even more than the smoldering promise in his eyes.

He was going to kiss her. She knew it even before he released her shoulders and cupped the back of her head, his fingers tangling in her hair. She willed herself to move, to break the spell of the moment before it was too late, but instead she let her eyes drift closed as he lowered his head and the whisper of his breath touched hers.

His lips were warm and soft and his beard tickled delicately as he brushed her mouth, his lips teasing as they set her pulse to racing. Her will of steel melted until she was leaning against his broad chest, her arms sliding around him so naturally, she didn't even notice.

Excitement flared through Trevor as he felt her relaxing beneath his touch. He took her lips more firmly, caressing them, then deepening the kiss as they parted beneath his. Her hands sent shivers through the muscles of his back and he had to fight to keep from turning the kiss into a full-blown seduction. Desire blazed inside him like a forest fire, setting his body to aching and his heart . . .

Shock and memories of Amanda cooled the violent flames. He eased back, still wanting Diana, but no longer completely lost in the delightful sensations kissing her had set in motion. He shouldn't be doing this, not yet, and not with Diana. They were supposed to be friends; she was going to help him with Crystal and he was going to help her find a job. Beyond that . . .

Oh, how he wanted to go beyond that. But he wasn't a hot-blooded kid anymore. Wanting didn't make it right. He had to think of the consequences, of the people who could be hurt by what he did—like Crystal and Diana herself. Reluctantly, he broke the tempting contact and stepped away from her.

The chill she felt had nothing to do with the night air. Diana shivered, fighting an urge to hug herself as her head swirled with confusion. What had happened? Why was he suddenly pulling away? Was it because she'd clung to him so shamelessly? What if he thought she was some kind of tramp? After all, he'd lived with Eileen, so why shouldn't he suspect that she . . .

She looked so stricken, it tore at him. "I . . . ah . . . Please don't think that I . . ." Trevor stopped, realizing that he didn't have a clue as to what he wanted to say. He wasn't going to apologize, because he really wasn't sorry that he'd kissed her; but he didn't want her to misunderstand or . . .

Diana forced herself to look up into his eyes and some of her anxiety fled. He looked every bit as confused and concerned as she felt. Definitely not like the marauding pirate he so often resembled. She managed a weak smile. "What do you say, we blame what just happened on the magic of a tropical night?"

Relief at her practical approach eased the moment. "Sounds right to me, if you include the fact that you are as charming and irresistible as the moonlight."

His sweet compliment forced her to be honest about her feelings. "And perhaps we're both a bit lonely and vulnerable."

"It has been a pretty emotional day." Trevor took her hand, grateful that she understood his need to pull back. He only wished that he could forget the way she'd felt in his arms, the heated magic of her lips opening beneath his. "Finding out that I have a daughter . . ."

Diana nodded, aware that he was being sensible, but somehow disappointed that he'd given up kissing her so easily. Being in his arms had felt so good, so right; she hadn't wanted it to end, a fact that should have worried her but didn't. Could she be developing a wayward romantic streak?

She was relieved when they were back in the well-lighted living room. As Trevor moved around, stirring up the embers and adding a log to the fire, she banished her erotic fantasies. From now on, she'd obviously have to avoid moonlit strolls with Trevor if she didn't want to make a fool of herself. He was just too tempting.

She shook her head, wondering how Eileen could have given him up so easily. Had her sister really wanted a modeling career more than a life with Trevor? Or had there been a choice for Eileen? Trevor's casualness when she'd mentioned Eileen certainly seemed to indicate that he, at least, hadn't viewed their relationship as terribly significant.

"Not in the mood for a movie?" Trevor's question snapped her attention back to the present and the quizzical expression on his face made her wonder if she'd missed something while she was lost in the past.

A blush stained her cheeks. "I'm sorry, I was thinking about something else. A movie would be fine."

"I've got a pretty good collection, so why don't you pick one." Trevor waved a hand at the shelves on his entertainment wall. "If there's anything you don't see, just let me know and I'll have Harlan send it out."

Diana scanned the first few cassettes, then gasped in delight. "Send for more? Are you kidding? This is a fabulous collection. It would take me months to watch every one I'd like to see."

The silence following her enthusiastic statement seemed deeper than the quiet before. Her cheeks burned again as she realized the implication of her words. "I mean, these are really special. I had no idea so many of my favorites were available on cassettes. It makes it hard to decide where to start. They all . . ." She stopped, aware that she was just making it worse.

Sensing her discomfort and wanting to give her some space, Trevor headed for the kitchen. "Would you like some coffee or maybe a glass of wine? Or I have microwave popcorn, if you're interested."

"Just coffee. If I keep eating like I did at dinner, I'm going to have to jog around the island several times a day just to stay in shape."

"That can be arranged; but I have to tell you, so far as I can see, there is nothing wrong with your shape." Trevor offered the compliment without thinking, then swallowed a sigh. He meant the words wholeheartedly, but he certainly didn't want her to think that he was making a move on her—especially after what had happened on their walk.

He shook his head, realizing again just how difficult the next few days were going to be. He'd been married far too long to remember how to behave as a single man. The brief fling of dating he'd indulged in after

Amanda's death had only left him spent and miserable and since then . . .

But Diana was different. Kissing her hadn't left him aching with loneliness for Amanda. A wry smile lifted his lips. Actually, kissing her had made him ache in a much more pleasant fashion. But the timing was wrong. He couldn't be attracted to Crystal's aunt, couldn't start thinking of her only as a woman; it would make everything too complicated.

Feeling uncharacteristically confused, he stepped back into the living room. Diana turned to face him with a smile that sent a jolt of electricity through him. He had a sudden suspicion that it was already getting too complicated and he hadn't a clue as to how to reverse the trend. Nor was he sure that he really wanted to reverse it. He hadn't felt so alive in months.

Diana woke with a smile, her heart as light as the golden glow of sunlight that spilled in through the window that faced the restless ocean. Memories of the evening she'd spent with Trevor filled her mind. Who would have guessed that he liked romantic old movies, the classic kind with snappy dialogue and sparks between the stars? And that just being with him could be so much fun?

She got up, stretching luxuriously, then yawning as she sniffed the air. Louise must already be here, for scents of baking filled the air. Her stomach rumbled as she grabbed her clothes and headed for the shower. It would never do to get used to this kind of life, but she meant to enjoy every moment she could before . . .

For a moment the glow of the day seemed to dim, then she pushed away any thoughts of leaving here— of leaving Trevor. She'd deal with that when the time came; meanwhile, she had a job to do. She had to make Crystal's visit here perfect. Even thinking about it made her stomach knot. She knew it wasn't going to be easy.

Trevor greeted her at the foot of the stairs. "It's

about time you came down," he teased, his eyes glowing with excitement. "I've already made a list of a dozen things we can do while Crystal's here. Louise has all sorts of suggestions. I need you to tell me what will appeal to her the most."

Diana swallowed a strange pang of disappointment. Had she really thought his enthusiasm was for her? The memories of his kiss that had haunted her dreams were just proof of her vulnerability and a good reason why she'd better tend to the business of helping Crystal. Anything else would be a serious mistake. She shook back her hair. "Coffee first, then the lists."

By mid-afternoon, she was sure that Crystal would have to stay on Bellington Cay a month just to try everything Trevor had in mind. As she finished changing for dinner, she no longer cared. Leaving paradise seemed like a lousy idea, anyway. She smoothed down the full, silky skirt of her dress and met her own gaze in the mirror. She scarcely recognized the woman she'd become after just two days here; but she definitely liked the change. She could hardly wait to explore the island nightlife.

Trevor was waiting at the foot of the stairs and his low whistle made her blush with pleasure. Thanks to Ken's constant criticism, it had been a long time since she'd felt really attractive. "I'm going to enjoy showing you off tonight." His gaze made her feel young and free.

"I'm looking forward to it. I haven't been out dancing for over a year."

"Nor have I. You might have to watch your toes at first. I'm out of practice." Trevor's chuckle held no sadness.

"We'll start slow," she promised, happy at this sign that his grief was ebbing.

"By the way, I meant to ask you, do you want to call your mother before dinner? I mean, shouldn't you let her know about me and what we have planned for Crystal's vacation?''

Diana stiffened, surprised by the change of subject. "Ah, no, I don't think so." She immediately noted the way his smile seemed to fade. *Why now?* she groaned mentally, wishing she'd given more thought to what she was going to tell her mother about all this. Aware that he was still watching her closely, she forced a weak smile. "Mom might worry about Crystal coming so far alone. I'd rather tell her afterward."

"Won't she wonder where Crystal's going to be spending her Thanksgiving vacation?" Trevor studied Diana closely. What was going on here? Was there something she hadn't told him? But what? Why wasn't she eager to call her mother, let her know that Crystal's future was secure?

"Crystal and I had already made plans to spend the time in Pleasant Valley, not Arizona, so Mom won't expect more than just a phone call." Diana turned away, unable to meet his probing gaze. Though what she said was true, his concerned expression made her feel as if she was lying.

How could she explain that she was just trying to protect him? That she had no idea how her mother was going to take his sudden involvement in Crystal's life, but that she was sure Mom would fight to keep him from getting too close to his daughter? For Mom things had always been black and white—Eileen was the innocent victim, Trevor Sinclair the evil villain who'd destroyed her perfect daughter's life and left a defenseless child under her protection.

"But I . . ." Trevor began, then stopped when he noticed the stiffness of Diana's movements as she walked past him. Was there something about her mother's illness that she hadn't told him? Could she be too ill to be told? Or was it something else? Could Diana still doubt his integrity and devotion to his daughter? He sighed. "I just want everyone to know how much

I care, that I would never have stayed away from Crystal if I'd known about her.''

The hurt in his voice stopped Diana in her tracks. ''I know that, Trevor, and I want to tell Mom, but now is not the time.''

''Okay. I guess I'm a little new to this family stuff. My own was never very close. Dad made all the decisions, at home as well as in his business empire; Mother was pretty busy with her various charity functions, so I just kept out of everyone's way as much as I could.'' He grinned to cover the odd feeling of loss that came from the words. ''I stayed out of trouble that way.''

Diana met his gaze, seeing not the strong man before her, but the lonely boy he'd been. Suddenly, she found it easy to understand how his father had managed to hide Eileen's condition from his son. A warm tide of sympathy made her want to take him in her arms and welcome him into her own somewhat untidy, but loving family.

Trevor winced as he recognized the sympathy in Diana's eyes. Lord, that was the last thing he'd expected. But then, he'd never told anyone that before—well, no one since Amanda. He must really be losing it. He turned away, ashamed of having let his feelings show. ''Fortunately, Amanda came from a close family that welcomed me in.''

Amanda! Her name banished the warm feelings like a cold draft and Diana welcomed the splash of reality. She'd better remember that Trevor was still grieving for the woman he'd loved or she'd end up getting hurt worse than Eileen had. One burning kiss signified nothing more than rampant hormones fueled by moonlight—lovely, but dangerous if repeated.

Diana searched through her befuddled brain for a new subject, but she kept getting sidetracked by images of last night. She was grateful when Louise emerged from the kitchen to tell them that dinner was ready. Crystal's arrival suddenly seemed a very long time off, especially when she wasn't sure how she was going to handle the next few hours with Trevor.

Oddly enough, her fears proved groundless. Trevor insisted that Louise join them for dinner, then offered to drive her home on their way to the resort. Could he be as uneasy as she? It seemed out of character for a man so obviously used to being in charge; but what other reason could there be? She wished devoutly that she understood men better. Or at all.

Her first glimpse of the Bellington Sands nightclub area further eased her fears. It was far from the seductive scene she'd pictured. The well-lit room was obviously the dining room; the tables simply moved back and the French doors opened to the wide terrace where the band played with more enthusiasm than elegance. The dancers ranged in age from giggling children to a number of elderly couples who swayed in a far gentler rhythm than the laughing teenagers who were showing off the latest steps.

"Do you think Crystal will like this?" Trevor asked as he guided her to a table on the far side of the room.

"She'll be fascinated."

"What about you?"

"I've never seen anything like it," Diana admitted. "It really looks like fun."

"That's what people come here for and that's what the residents like, too. That's what I enjoy most about the island. The tourist trade is important, but the islanders haven't lost the feeling that this is their home and they're just welcoming invited guests." He waved to several groups in answer to shouts of greeting and Diana didn't miss the honest friendship that seemed to exist between him and his island neighbors.

"I can understand why you're so happy here." For a moment she ached, already dreading the time when she and Crystal would have to catch the interisland plane for their return.

Trevor swallowed a sigh as he signaled one of the

busy barmaids. Happy here? Though he had no intention of telling her, he knew only too well that hadn't been true before Thursday night. He'd been reasonably content here; happiness had come when he'd offered shelter to a dazed and shaky stranger.

"Are you ready to risk the dance floor?" he asked, suddenly sure that he didn't want to talk about his feelings. He knew he wasn't ready to handle real happiness or the risk of heartbreak that came with caring.

"I'm a gambler, why not?" Diana got to her feet at once, excited by the prospect of being in his arms, yet anxious, too, for she didn't like the sensation of losing her emotional control that seemed to come over her every time Trevor so much as touched her hand. Her own words taunted her—she'd never been a gambler. In fact, she'd prided herself on being cautious, on always thinking before she acted, on making rational choices instead of emotional ones.

As his arm slipped around her, she pushed all such thoughts from her mind and just enjoyed the illusion of gliding through a dream as they moved across the spacious dance floor toward the open doors. She had no trouble following Trevor's firm lead except on the turns when her body brushed his and a seductive dizziness threatened her balance.

"I guess dancing is a lot like swimming and riding a bike—you never forget how," Trevor murmured, his warm breath tickling her cheek. "Only this is a lot more fun."

"It sure is." She sounded breathless, but she no longer cared. Like the islanders, she wanted only to enjoy the night. It seemed a lifetime since she'd just had fun. Tomorrow would be soon enough to worry about the future.

It was well after two A.M. when Trevor opened the front door for her. Diana yawned and stretched lazily. "That was great. I can't remember the last time I danced so much."

"Didn't your husband take you dancing?" The question was out before he thought and he instantly regretted it. Though he might be curious about the man Diana had married, he'd had no intention of ruining the evening by mentioning him.

"Ken wasn't much for nightclubs." Diana felt her pleasure draining away, leaving behind only weariness. "I'm sure Crystal will love going out and meeting all your friends."

"I'll enjoy showing her off." Trevor cursed himself for taking the glow of happiness from her eyes. He tried to think of a way to bring it back. "Would you like a glass of wine? We could light a fire and . . ."

And sit snuggled together on the couch. Her mind supplied the appropriate images and a shaft of longing tore through her. She forced herself to shake her head. Leaning on Trevor for emotional support was the last thing she needed to do. "I think I'd better drag myself upstairs while I still can. All that dancing . . ." She murmured her thanks, then fled from the temptation posed by the longing that she could see in his eyes.

Trevor watched her go with an odd mixture of relief and disappointment. Being near her was a delightful torment, but was he being fair to himself or to her? It surprised him to realize that he really wasn't sure. Holding her close on the dance floor, watching her laugh and talk with all his friends had seemed right and natural; but now . . . He locked the door and turned out the lights. It was definitely time to call it a night.

Sunday and Monday passed pleasantly. Trevor took Diana out for a morning cruise on the island's only rental deep-sea fishing boat; then they explored the nearby islands in his powerboat and fished for their dinner in one of the coves. According to Trevor, they were testing each adventure for Crystal, who was due to arrive on Wednesday; but just being with Trevor made it a time of enchantment for Diana.

Each shared experience brought them closer as they

talked and laughed together. She told him dozens of stories about growing up in Pleasant Valley and about Crystal's life there, as well as her own, while he gave her a glimpse of his challenging and exciting world of business and power. Only two subjects were ignored. He said little about Amanda, except for mentioning how valuable she'd been to the company they'd created and shared, and she never mentioned Ken.

Only one small disagreement marred the perfection of the days and evenings they spent together—Trevor's continued desire for her to call her mother, and the guilt she felt each time he brought up the subject. She knew he was right. Mom did have a right to know, but there was so much to be explained since Diana hadn't even told her mother about the lack of money or her plan to ask Trevor for help.

Besides, how could she tell her mother something so mind-blowing long distance? What if Mom got so angry she had trouble breathing? Or decided to forbid Crystal to come? If she was being a coward, so be it. She just couldn't risk it, not yet.

By Tuesday evening everything was in order. The guest room was ready, and the refrigerator fairly bulged with all the goodies Louise had prepared. Trevor had insisted that she help him select an island wardrobe for Crystal, all of which was now spread out in colorful splendor on what soon would be Crystal's bed. Diana sighed as she studied the generous gifts and thought of all that she'd talked him out of buying.

Crystal would be overwhelmed. Or would she? What if she was crazy about everything and wanted to stay on forever, instead of going back to school or even on to Wilding in the fall? What if she fell under Trevor's spell and never wanted to see her family again?

A chill chased down Diana's spine. There'd been a time when she wouldn't have believed that possible, but then she'd once believed that marriage was forever and she was now a divorcée. Not that the two were in any way related, except for the distance that had grown between her and Crystal in the months since her marriage had ended.

"Diana?" A tap on the door forced the dark thoughts away, and Diana turned from the clothing display to see Trevor standing in the guest room doorway. "Is there something else we should put in here?"

She found his worried frown endearing. "I can't imagine what else she could need. She's going to be here only four days, Trevor, not a month."

"I just want her to be happy."

His anxiety tore at her, but it also worried her and she felt she had to warn him. "Getting to know her father will take care of that, but she'll need time, Trevor. Don't try to overwhelm her with gifts and things. You can't buy her love."

"Is that really what you think I'm trying to do?" The anger in his face shocked her. "But then, why wouldn't you? That was why you came here, wasn't it? You wanted money from me."

"That was before I knew . . ." The unfairness of his accusation brought a pain so sharp, she couldn't finish the sentence.

"And now you know, you still don't trust me enough to call anyone or tell the world that Crystal has a father. Are you hoping that this meeting will go so badly that Crystal won't ever want to see me again? Then you'd have what you came for, my support and no interference."

A sob of anguish swelled in her throat, then dissolved under a rising tide of anger. "If I wanted this visit to fail, why would I stay and help? Crystal didn't even want to come until I assured her that I'd be here with her the whole time. As for calling anyone, you don't know what you're asking. Why can't you just trust my judgment and . . ." Words failed her as her stomach knotted and the food she'd eaten for dinner burned in the back of her throat.

"What do you mean Crystal didn't want to come? And why is it too much to ask you to tell your mother that I'm not the villain who ruined everyone's life?" The mingling of shock and pain in his face shattered her protective anger and she suddenly knew she couldn't face him, not now.

She stumbled through the connecting bath to her room, but she could hear him behind her, calling her name. He wasn't going to give up, she realized, then grabbed her sweater and slipped out the French doors to the upper deck and quickly made her way down the outside staircase. The moonlit sand beckoned and she set off at an easy lope, not even looking back.

Trevor paused outside her bedroom door, taking deep breaths, trying hard to control his temper. He'd spoken in anger, not really believing his own accusations; but now he wasn't so sure. Had trusting Diana been a mistake? She seemed so open and kind and loving, but what if she really did want him to fail? He had to talk to her, had to find out why she wanted her presence here to remain a secret from everyone but Crystal.

"Diana, please talk to me. We can't leave it like this. I need to know why you don't trust me."

Silence echoed through the empty house. He knocked on the door, gently at first, then harder, finally twisting the knob. To his surprise, the door opened easily. The room was empty and the French doors were open to the night air.

Swearing, he crossed the room and stepped out on the deck. It took him only a moment to spot her as she ran along the sand. She was running away from him. Without giving it a second thought, he ran lightly down the stairs and set off in pursuit.

Diana slowed, her breath coming in sobbing gusts. How could she have let it happen again? Would she never learn not to trust her judgment about men? But how could she have been so wrong about Trevor?

Or was she wrong? Now that her anger was spent,

she had to admit that it had been partly fueled by her own guilt over not calling her mother. But why couldn't he trust her as he'd expected her to trust him? Why couldn't it be as it had been earlier when they'd laughed and planned and . . .

She stopped, fighting her tears as she looked around. A bitter laugh rose in her throat as she realized exactly where she was. The moonlit beauty of Hibiscus Cove shimmered around her.

"Diana." Trevor's voice was rather hoarse, but startlingly near at hand.

She straightened up, ignoring the pain in her side, the burning in her chest, and the ache in her heart. She dared not let him see her longing, for she knew that she'd never be able to resist him if he took her in his arms again. "What are you doing here?"

"Please, we have to talk. You have to tell me what's wrong. You say I don't understand about your family, but you won't tell me and . . ." He stopped, frowning as though he wasn't exactly sure what he wanted to say.

Diana closed her eyes, trying to escape the guilt she still felt. She could feel the heat of shame in her cheeks as she explained. "I'm afraid to call Mom, Trevor, afraid of what she'll say and how she'll feel. You've been the enemy to her for seventeen years; one phone call isn't going to be enough to convince her. If I call her now, she could refuse to let Crystal come. That's why I haven't told her."

"She hates me that much?" The pain in his voice forced her to look at him again.

"She hates the man who denied Eileen and her child; the man she still blames for Eileen's death." She winced from the words, feeling his pain and hating herself for inflicting it even while she felt the worst of her guilt easing.

"But when you tell her . . ."

"At the moment Mom seems to be having trouble

trusting my judgment.'' Diana turned away, gazing out at the moon-kissed waves that danced in the cove. ''She might not believe me.''

''Why not?''

''That's not important. What matters is that you and Crystal have a chance to get acquainted during her Thanksgiving vacation. After that, I swear I'll shout the truth from the rooftops if that's what you want.'' She met his gaze, hoping that he'd understand, that he'd give her time and space before he demanded more answers than she had to give. She didn't want to think about the past now, not when the future seemed to hold so much promise.

SIX

Trevor felt the weight shifting from his shoulders as her words broke through the doubt that had clouded his mind on the long run. She did care. She wanted tomorrow's meeting to be a success just as much as he did. Relief spread over him like a healing breeze on a hot afternoon. Suddenly he was very conscious of the way her breasts rose and fell beneath the light knit of her cotton sweater.

She looked so vulnerable, so tentative, as though she thought he might hurt her. Lord, what had happened to her? What kind of torment had she been subjected to that would reduce her to near timidity? He'd seen flashes of her temper and her spirit during the past few days, so he knew that she had pride and strength and fire; but now . . . He couldn't bear it.

Without a word, he caught her hand and drew her closer to him, close enough so that he could even see the pulse that beat at the base of her throat, so that he could catch the scent of sandalwood that drifted from her hair as the evening breeze tore the burnished tendrils free of her combs, tempting him to tangle his fingers in their softness.

"Please don't run away from me, Diana. Don't you

know that I'd never hurt you or Crystal? I just didn't understand and that bothered me. I guess I'm too used to being in charge and with this I . . .'' Words failed him as he lost himself in the wonder of her eyes. Her soft lips were so close, so tempting.

The warning voice sounded inside her, but Diana paid no attention. How could she when the moonlight threw fascinating patterns of light and shadow on the face of the man before her, when his strong fingers caressed hers with such tenderness, spreading delicate quivers of desire through her.

Desire? There was no other word for it. It came from the slumberous glow of moonlight in his eyes as they focused on her lips and from the touch of his hand as he gently wound his fingers in her hair, cupping the back of her head as he moved closer, his eyes holding her willing prisoner even as her lips parted to welcome his kiss.

He freed her fingers as he drew her closer, and she explored the rippling muscles of his back and discovered the damp curls on the nape of his neck. Pirate's curls, springy and intriguing as she caressed the warm skin they covered, glorying in the wild fire of his demanding lips, his plundering tongue.

It was heaven to lean against his broad chest, to feel his strong arms around her, holding her close as he explored the depths of her mouth and filled her senses with the mingled scents of his tangy after-shave and his own musky maleness. She wanted to lose herself forever in the magic, to forget everything but the wonder of surrendering to . . .

Madness! Diana froze, fighting the wild sensations that threatened to overwhelm her. This had to be insanity. There was no other explanation for her behavior. She shuddered as Trevor's lips left hers to trace a burning trail across her cheek and down the side of her neck. She willed herself to pull away, to fight the delicious weakness that seemed to have invaded her body;

but she only clung to him more tightly, moaning as he nipped gently at her earlobe.

When his lips reclaimed hers, she answered him with a wild abandon she'd never known before. For an eternity, she gloried in the swirling passion, the proof that, in spite of Ken's furious accusations, she could feel and want and love . . .

Love. The word swept through her with chilling force and this time she couldn't deny reality. Slowly, sadly, she released the stunning dream and forced herself to step back, to leave the haven of his arms. Her breath came in sobs far more painful than her gasping from the long run. "We have to stop, Trevor."

Trevor moaned, fighting an almost irresistible urge to drag her back against him. He couldn't let her go, not now when he'd felt the fire raging between them, the pliant promise of her body against his. Not when he needed so desperately to . . .

Sanity washed away the clinging tendrils of passion, leaving his overheated body chilled by the realization of what he was thinking and feeling. He swallowed hard, then took a deep breath, but it didn't help. He still wanted her, ached for her. And when their eyes met, he knew that she still wanted him.

"This is wrong, Trevor." Saying the words hurt, but it was her only defense against her own desire. "We have to think about tomorrow, about Crystal and . . ." She stopped, unwilling to admit her own weakness, her own desperate need to be loved. He was a man just past grieving and still in love with his dead wife; she had no right to take advantage of him now.

Shaken by the realization of how close he'd come to seducing her right here on the beach, Trevor ran a shaking hand through his hair. "I'm sorry, Diana, I never meant for it to get so . . . intense." Bitter amusement filled him—that was certainly the understatement of the century, unless he considered a volcano intense.

But where had the passion come from? One moment

he'd wanted to comfort her, to assure her that he meant her no harm, and the next he'd been ready to rip off her clothes and ravish her just like the pirates of old. And she hadn't exactly been fighting him off. He studied her closely, his heart contracting painfully as he recognized his own confusion in her eyes.

"It was my fault, too." Her lower lip was quivering, like that of a child about to cry. "I don't know what came over me. I've never just let go this way. I'm really not that kind of person. It must be this place or the night or . . ." She seemed to run out of words, but she didn't look away and her heart shone from her eyes—a vulnerable heart that could be so easily bruised or broken.

He ignored his own desire to reassure her. "You're a wonderful person, Diana. What happened tonight is just the result of all the emotions that have been stirred up since you told me about Crystal. We've both been lonely, so I suppose it's not surprising that we should feel something toward each other. I'm sure everything will be fine as soon as Crystal arrives."

"Of course it will." She tried hard to match his conviction, but it wasn't easy since she had a strong suspicion that nothing in her life would ever be quite the same again. In spite of her protests, she already knew that her reaction to his kiss had nothing to do with moonlight or loneliness.

"So shall we go home?" He took her hand, wanting to hold her close again but aware that he had no right. Whatever had caused her divorce had left her too vulnerable; he couldn't take advantage of her—no matter how much he wanted her.

"Do you really think I bought too much for Crystal?" he asked, more to distract himself than because he was really worried.

"No, I'm sure she'll love everything." Diana smiled at him, relieved by the change of subject. Then her thoughts turned serious as she remembered her earlier worries. She didn't want to anger him, but there was so much he needed to know about his daughter. "It's just that I know you're tempted to try to give her everything that you didn't have a chance to give her before and I don't want her to think of you that way—as someone who just gives and requires nothing in return."

"I don't understand." His sharp tone told her that she'd been right to expect resentment. "Why should I expect anything from her?"

"As her father, you have a right to her respect and love; but because of the circumstances, she may not be willing to offer either one."

"I can understand that."

"So can I, but what I'm saying is that you can't allow her to take advantage of your desire to win her over. She may look and act like an adult, but in many ways she's still a child and she needs to learn that other people have feelings, too. I'm afraid consideration and unselfishness are learned, not natural." She swallowed a sigh, remembering how many times she'd hurt her own mother without realizing it. It was only recently that she'd begun to understand that love could be cruel as well as healing.

"So what am I supposed to do?" Trevor's frown told her that he was still having trouble understanding.

"Treat her as you would a new friend. Someone you're disposed to like, but not required to. If she acts like a brat, let her see that you can be hurt or angered by it. Don't pamper her. She can make your life hell, if you let her." Diana didn't bother to hide her feelings this time; protecting both Crystal and Trevor was too important.

Awareness dawned in Trevor's mind. "She's hurt you a lot, hasn't she?"

Diana sighed. "Not intentionally, but, yes, she has. We're still working it out, which is why I wanted to warn you. Just don't take everything she says or does to heart. Teenagers tend to have the attention span of a gnat and are as changeable as a chameleon on plaid.''

"Teenager.'' Trevor shuddered. "That's scary, you know.''

"Especially since you missed the easy years.'' Her heart ached for him. "I'm really sorry, Trevor, both for you and for Crystal. She's needed a father for a long time and I think you'll be a good one.''

"If I get the chance.'' Her words had chilled him, making the pitfalls ahead only too real. His fingers tightened on her hand. Thank God he wasn't facing tomorrow alone.

"That's what this vacation is all about.'' Her voice was soft, gentle, but the promise was strong. "It's a chance for both of you.''

By the time Trevor drove to the island airstrip, Diana was making the transition from frantic to basket case. Though she'd spent most of the day reassuring him that everything was going to be fine, she hadn't believed a word of it. She just knew this visit was going to explode in her face. Crystal would hate Trevor and her for letting him into her life and her mother . . . Diana couldn't even imagine what her mother was going to say when she found out what Diana had set in motion.

Only one thought consoled her—Crystal couldn't run away. Once she got off the plane, she was here until tomorrow morning's flight. Unless she found out about the interisland ferry. But then, thanks to Louise, half the island knew that Crystal was coming, so she'd never be able to sneak away.

"Are you really that worried?'' Trevor's question broke into her dark thoughts, reminding her that she wasn't alone in her fears.

"I just want everything to go well, that's all.''

"We've done all we can. The rest is up to Crystal.'' He sounded so firm and together, she hated him, until she realized that his knuckles were white from the death grip he had on the steering wheel.

"I'm sure she's going to love it here." She could say that with confidence, since Crystal had spent a good bit of last summer at the beach home of her Cliffton roommate. It was a defection that Diana still resented; she'd desperately needed a friend last summer and Crystal had been nowhere around.

The island airport came as a shock, since the only visible structure was a battered wooden building about the size of a carnival booth, which contained little more than a counter and a pay telephone. To Diana's surprise Eban was there with the island taxi, as were representatives from both the resorts, not to mention several local families.

"Are we late?" Diana asked as Trevor parked along the rough track that pretended to be a road. What if Crystal had arrived to find no one waiting?

Trevor shook his head. "We would have heard the plane."

"Oh."

He was already out, moving around the car to open the door for her, but she couldn't move. Her legs felt numb and her head was beginning to pound. She was going to be . . . A distant sound penetrated her panic attack.

"See, I told you." Trevor's wide grin made it clear that the noise was the approaching plane.

Her heart did a slow roll, then hit warp speed. He looked like a kid awaiting Santa's arrival. While he scanned the sky for the plane, she slipped from the car and shrugged the tension from her shoulders. This had to work—Trevor deserved a chance and so did Crystal. She'd make it work—if it killed them! Courage firmly in hand, she moved to Trevor's side.

Hugs, introductions, and luggage claiming filled the first few moments after Crystal stepped out of the small plane, but all too soon, it was time to leave. "Would you like to drive around the island, Crystal, or would you rather go straight to the house?'' Trevor's smile was polite, but Diana could see the lines of strain deepening at the corners of his eyes, the stiffness in his movements.

Crystal shrugged, then dove into the backseat of the car, making it clear that she didn't want to sit beside her father. Diana swallowed a sigh, trying to offer Trevor a reassuring smile across the top of the car. Obviously, this wasn't going to be easy.

Not anxious to be alone with Crystal at the house, she decided to buy some time. ''I think we should drive around, let Crystal see how really beautiful Bellington Cay is.''

To her surprise, the suggestion proved to be a good one. Trevor relaxed a little as he entertained Crystal with anecdotes about the places and people on the island. His obvious love of both gave a warmth to his voice that Diana found irresistible; it even helped her to join in, further easing the strain. By the time they finally reached the house, she was beginning to believe the visit was going to work.

''Want to hit the beach before dinner?'' she asked as they got out of the car.

''I'll have to if I'm going to match your tan.'' Crystal's grin was wicked. ''Now I know why you didn't want to come home right away.''

Diana felt the immediate heat of embarrassment in her cheeks and turned away from Crystal's bright gaze. ''Could you resist all this white sand and blue ocean?'' No way could she let Crystal even suspect that getting to know Trevor had been her real reason for staying.

''It really could be paradise.'' A sudden note of longing in Crystal's voice brought Diana around, and when she looked at her niece, Diana realized that the girl's gaze was directed at Trevor, not the beach.

So Crystal did care. Relief swept through Diana. Her niece had been so cool and cynical, both on the phone and after her arrival, that Diana had begun to wonder if this meeting had come too late; but now she knew there was hope. Crystal wanted a father every bit as much as Trevor wanted his daughter.

"You wouldn't be talking about paradise if you were here in August," Trevor broke in as he lifted Crystal's suitcases out of the trunk. "The air gets so humid you have to hack your way through it and nothing ever dries out. Even the mildew gets mildew."

Crystal's giggle sounded wonderfully familiar. "So why stay? I thought Diana said you were from Denver. It's got to be cooler there."

"Good point." Trevor headed for the door. "Come on, I'll show you your room."

Diana followed them slowly, wondering if she'd been wise to leave out so much when she told Crystal about her father. She just hadn't known how Crystal would take the news that her father had married someone else instead of Eileen. Of course, now that Crystal was here, she'd have to know—and the sooner the better.

Well, maybe not too soon, she amended as she heard a squeal of delight from the other guest bedroom. Obviously Crystal had discovered the gifts piled on her bed. By the time Diana arrived, her niece was already parading in front of the mirror as she tried to decide which of her new bathing suits to try on first.

Trevor positively glowed with satisfaction as he promised to meet them on the beach as soon as they were changed. Diana closed the door behind him and took a deep breath, not sure how to begin or what to say.

"So where's your room?" Crystal asked, her smile fading slightly now that they were alone.

"We share the bath." Diana pointed toward the partly open door. "Do you like the clothes?"

"What's not to like? They're awesome. You helped him pick them out, didn't you?"

Diana nodded. "You're the first seventeen-year-old he's ever shopped for."

"Does he think I'm going to be here long enough to wear them all?" Crystal was looking down at the bright-colored shorts and shirts, but the tension in her slender body made it clear that her thoughts weren't really on the clothes.

"I think he hopes this will just be the first of many visits. He wants you to be a part of his life, Crystal, and to be a part of yours."

"He can pay my tuition to Wilding." Her tone was bitter and her gaze frosty when she glanced at Diana.

"He wants more than that. He feels cheated because his father kept him from knowing you. He wants a daughter, not a tax deduction." She kept her words flat, unemotional. "That's why you're here."

"On approval?"

Diana groaned and cast her gaze toward the ceiling, clearly recognizing the cynicism that Jennifer, Crystal's roommate, exuded. With a mother who changed husbands regularly, Jennifer's attitude was understandable; but Diana wished mightily that she hadn't let it spill over onto Crystal. "He's not buying you, Crystal. He wants to get to know you. He wants to be there for you and help you and have fun with you."

Crystal said nothing, just sifted through the clothes again, finally selecting a brilliant emerald green bikini. "So go change and we'll have some fun."

Diana hesitated for a moment, wanting to say more, yet unsure how to handle this much-loved stranger. Finally, she gave up. Maybe she was worrying too much; maybe she should just let Trevor and Crystal work things out themselves and . . . And pick up the pieces if things went wrong? The prospect made the knot in her stomach worse but brought her no answers.

She'd barely pulled on her sapphire suit when Crystal tapped on the bathroom door. "This look okay?" she asked, tugging at the narrow pieces of fabric and looking anxious.

"You look lovely," Diana assured her, understanding only too well her niece's doubts and insecurity, thanks to the misery of her marriage to Ken. There was nothing harder than trying to please someone when you had no idea what it was they expected from you. "Trevor will be impressed."

"I just want to get some sun before the day is over." Crystal grabbed one of the beach towels Diana had laid out and headed for the French door. "Can we get down from here?"

"The stairs are at the end of the deck." Diana picked up the sunscreen and her own towel and slipped her feet into her thongs. Obviously Crystal wasn't ready to admit that she cared what her father thought.

That brief exchange seemed to set the pattern for the rest of the afternoon. Crystal alternated between chattering flirtatiously with Trevor and a moody withdrawal in which she ignored both Diana and Trevor. It was an emotional seesaw that Diana could do nothing about, though she could see it was driving Trevor half crazy.

Dinner brought a brief respite, mostly thanks to Louise's friendly presence and her promise to introduce Crystal to some of the island teenagers before tomorrow's big Thanksgiving dinner. The rest of the evening they filled with videos and popcorn. By the time she followed Crystal up the wrought-iron staircase, the tension had Diana wondering if they could survive the strain for four whole days.

Trevor moved slowly across the living room, picking up the discarded bowls, cups, and glasses. Why had Diana gone up with Crystal? Didn't she realize how badly he needed to talk to her? He needed her insight into the complicated stranger who looked so much like Eileen she filled his mind with long-forgotten memories and worried him to death. He couldn't help wondering if Crystal was as flighty as Eileen—and worrying that she might drift out of his life just as her mother had.

But he wouldn't let her, he told himself firmly. Eileen had been a free spirit, but Crystal belonged to him and he meant to make sure she knew that before she left the island. The question was, how did he do that? How could he make her care about him? He cast a longing gaze up the stairs, but Diana wasn't at the top and, with Crystal in the next room, there was no way he could go upstairs and tap on her door.

Frustrated and still too wired to settle down, Trevor let himself out into the cooling night. Maybe a run on the beach would clear his head. He set off at a slow jog, wishing mightily that Diana was beside him. He sighed and shook his head, wondering when she'd become so important to him—and what that might mean in the future. Or if they even had a future.

Diana stood in the dark, staring out the French doors at the moonlit sand. Weariness hung heavy over her shoulders, yet she longed for something . . . A dark shadow moved smoothly along the pale sand and her heart leaped. Trevor. Though she couldn't really see him, she didn't doubt his identity. She closed her eyes, wishing that she could join him, wishing that it was last night and she was in his arms again.

Cursing her own foolishness, she stepped back from the French doors and glanced toward the bathroom. She would need all her wits about her now that Crystal was here, which meant she'd better stop daydreaming about Trevor and get some sleep. Tomorrow would be an important day in Crystal's and Trevor's lives, so she had to make it right, somehow.

There was not a lot to be thankful for so far this Thanksgiving Day, Diana decided as she took refuge in the downstairs bath. The traditional Thanksgiving dinner that she and Louise had planned so carefully had been eaten in near silence thanks to Crystal's pouting.

And now, while Louise was putting the final touches on the pumpkin and mincemeat pies, Crystal was insisting that she wanted to call her grandmother.

Which really shouldn't be a surprise, Diana reminded herself. She'd known that they'd have to call today. Only she'd hoped that it would be later, maybe in the evening after a day of family warmth and closeness. Unfortunately, they'd awakened to rain so hard Crystal couldn't visit Louise's house to spend the early afternoon swimming with some of the island teenagers; a disaster for which Crystal had, with pure teenage logic, decided to blame Trevor and Diana.

Diana rubbed her temples, well aware that nothing but time would ease her headache. Time and Mom's forgiveness. She sighed. No way could she endure a headache that long—which meant she'd better come up with the right words when she got on the phone to Arizona. Her stomach turned the turkey with all the trimmings into a solid granite lump. She had a strong suspicion that there were no right words.

A rap on the door startled her out of her worrying. "Grandma wants to talk to you now, Diana." Crystal sounded almost cheerful.

"I thought you were going to wait until after dinner," Diana mumbled as she opened the door and stepped into the kitchen.

"Louise said the pies would keep."

The wall phone was off the hook, waiting. Diana approached it with caution. "Happy Thanksgiving, Mom," she began.

It was nearly five long minutes before she was allowed to speak again and that was only because her mother was coughing and needed to stop for breath. Diana swallowed hard, then plunged in, stating her reasons for coming and her discoveries about Trevor in unemotional terms, finishing, "Since he had no way of knowing of Crystal's existence until I told him, I thought it only fair that he have a chance to meet his daughter. After all, he . . .''

''He destroyed her mother's life, so you thought you should let him ruin Crystal's, too?'' Her mother had regained her voice.

''I told you, Mom, Eileen left Trevor before she knew she was pregnant. Everything after that was his father's doing, not Trevor's. All he wants is to help his daughter.''

''He wants her, period, mark my words. And you handed her over to him. He can give her the moon. What makes you think she'll ever want to be with us? You messed up your own life with your divorce, so now you're going to deprive me of my only grandchild, too. How could you?''

Protests at the vicious attack rose in her throat, but Diana was suddenly conscious of Trevor and Louise just a room away and Crystal standing at her shoulder, listening to every word. She took a deep breath, controlling her temper. ''This is something we'll have to discuss in person, Mom, so why don't you just think over what I've told you and we'll talk when I get to Phoenix, okay?''

Silence hummed over the line for so long she wondered if her mother had hung up; then she heard a weary sigh that nearly broke her heart. ''You haven't given me much choice, have you?''

''When I found out about the trust being gone, I didn't feel I had much choice.'' Diana held her head high, wishing mightily that she felt as confident as she sounded. As confident as she'd been before her mistake of a marriage had started her questioning every decision she made.

''You could have asked me.'' Her mother's voice was softer now, heavy with worry. ''Well, it's done, so you'll have to live with whatever happens. And so will Crystal and I. Let me talk to her again.''

Diana handed over the telephone, then stepped out

on the back porch, preferring the chill rain to the warm kitchen. Had she made a mistake? Had her attraction to Trevor led her to risk Crystal's happiness? She didn't want to think so, but she'd once thought Ken Foster was a kind and honorable man who truly loved her, a belief that had proved painfully incorrect.

"You can come back in now." Crystal's voice brought her around, but the real shock came from the expression on her niece's lovely face. Crystal was grinning. "You really should have told her sooner, you know."

It was cards on the table time, Diana realized. She'd skirted the truth with everyone for long enough. "I was afraid she'd forbid you to come."

"Did you think that would stop me?" Crystal's grin curdled a little.

"I didn't know. You sounded kind of doubtful when I invited you, so I didn't want to risk it. I thought you had a right to meet your father, get to know him. And I wanted him to meet you, to see just how much you deserve a chance to attend Wilding."

Diana waited, expecting Crystal to say more, but she just shrugged and turned away. "Let's go eat some pie. Arguing with Grandma always gives me an appetite."

It also seemed to change her attitude, Diana noticed as the long day drizzled to an end. The sullen, angry Crystal had vanished and in her place was the sweet young girl Diana had adored from the day Eileen brought her into her life. The reasons behind Crystal's transformation worried her, but not so much she couldn't enjoy the blessings of peace while they lasted. Besides, watching Trevor relax into the role of happy father was enough to make her forget everything else.

When Friday dawned sunny, Diana's feeling of hope grew, and by the time Crystal left with Louise to spend the afternoon on the beach with the island teenagers, she was convinced that everything was going to work out after all. She was anxious to share the feeling with

Trevor because she knew they'd have little time alone after tomorrow. Trevor had informed them both that they would all three have to go to Nassau on the plane in the morning and stay overnight there so Crystal could make her early flight back to the States. Diana knew she should also be taking that flight, though she had no desire to leave paradise. Or was it Trevor she couldn't bear to leave?

She hurried inside after her stroll on the beach and followed the sound of his voice up the stairs to the door of his office. "Yeah, Harlan, I think it's really going to work out. She's a dynamite kid; pretty as her mother and bright . . ."

Diana paused, not wanting to eavesdrop but too curious to retreat to the living room.

"Now don't go getting notions like that." Trevor's chuckle kept her in place. "This is just about my being a father, I told you that. Diana has been like a mother to Crystal, so she's been closer to her than anyone else. Don't start inventing a romance." His cold tone chilled away her pleasure.

Trevor was talking about her and it didn't take a genius to figure out what his friend and partner Harlan Cole had said. Harlan must have accused Trevor of being interested in her as well as in his daughter. And Trevor had denied it vehemently.

Embarrassment burned in her cheeks. Suddenly sure that she couldn't allow him to know she'd overheard him, Diana turned and tiptoed back down the stairs. What else had Trevor told his friend? Had he made her unannounced arrival here into an amusing tale? And what about the kisses they'd shared? Had Trevor forgotten them now that he had Crystal?

Lord, but he must think her an unsophisticated fool, mooning around here, babbling about paradise. Holding hands with him in the dark, clinging to him as though she were love-starved when he kissed her at Hibiscus

Cove. She leaned against the kitchen counter, blinking back the tears that burned in her eyes.

"Diana, where are you?" Trevor's voice echoed through the empty house. "I've made all kinds of plans for tomorrow."

She wanted to run, to race along the beach until she was too tired to feel the pain; but, of course, she couldn't. There was no place to hide on Bellington Cay, no way she could escape the consequences of her own actions. Or the vulnerability of her heart.

SEVEN

Trevor paused at the foot of the stairs; then the soft sound of water running in the kitchen drew his attention. He stepped into the sunlit room, his excitement doubled by the thought of sharing it with her. "Diana, wait till you hear what we're going to be doing in Nassau."

"What now?" She was at the sink, washing something, her back toward him.

"I was worried about finding hotel rooms, but I just talked to a friend of mine and he's going to let us stay in his beach house. He'll loan us a car, too, so we can explore the island or drive into Nassau so you can go shopping, whichever you two want to do." It took all his self-control not to just go over and take her in his arms. In fact, he'd had trouble keeping his hands off her ever since those magic moments at Hibiscus Cove; but with Crystal here, he couldn't risk it. His daughter was finally beginning to be friendly toward him.

"That sounds nice."

"I just want things to go smoothly now that Crystal is starting to accept me as her father." Trevor's euphoria ebbed quickly. Something was wrong, he could feel it. "She is beginning to trust me, isn't she?"

Diana took a deep breath, then swallowed her own misery. This was no time to think about herself, not when she could hear the doubts returning to Trevor's voice. She forced a smile, then turned to meet his gaze. "I think it's going great. She's really enjoying herself."

"I was getting pretty worried yesterday," he admitted, leaning his broad shoulders against the door frame, his expression grave as he studied her. "Then all of a sudden, she just seemed to come alive and since then . . ."

Looking into his eyes sent a current of electricity through her, set her pulse to racing with a longing for so much more. The ache inside her deepened, but she forced herself to ignore it. "That's teenagers for you. Their moods go up and down more often than a yo-yo. I'll talk to her on the flight back and make sure that she's comfortable with everything, but I'm sure . . ." She let it trail off, suddenly aware of the change in his mood as he came toward her.

"What do you mean—on the flight back? You can't leave with her on Sunday."

"What do you mean, I can't leave?" Her stomach knotted, but she wasn't sure whether it was anger or excitement that pulsed through her.

"I mean, there's no reason for you to go yet. We have so many plans to make and so much that I still need to know about financing her schooling at Wilding and all her other needs." He spoke quickly, trying to cover his feelings. The financial questions could be handled simply enough—he'd already set much of the paperwork in motion during his conversation with Harlan—but the prospect of watching Diana leave with Crystal had hit him a lot harder than he'd expected. Even considering it made him ache with loneliness.

"But I have to go back, Trevor. I need to check on the sale of the shop and then I should fly down to Phoenix and talk to Mom. She was terribly upset and she's not going to relax until I convince her that you're not the enemy." She did her best to ignore the fact that her words lacked conviction.

"Just a few more days? You probably wouldn't be able to get on the plane anyway. There'll be lots of people leaving Sunday. If you wait until mid-week . . ." He let it trail off, suddenly sure that he wouldn't want her to go then either.

"Well, if you really think I should stay . . ." Looking into his eyes, seeing the honest need there, she couldn't refuse. Maybe she'd misunderstood what she'd overheard. Maybe Trevor felt the same longing that tormented her. Maybe . . . maybe she was the biggest fool in the world; but if there was a chance that he really did feel something for her, she had to stay.

Trevor looked down at her, losing himself in her wide blue eyes. Guileless eyes, that was what a poet would call them, full of innocence and honesty and so tempting, like her lips. Desire flooded through him, making him ache to explore the blazing heat that suddenly seemed to fill the kitchen. A bone-deep hunger made him reach out to touch her cheek, to tangle his fingers in her unruly mane.

He did feel it, too! Her heart beat faster under the spur of the passion that flamed in his eyes. His touch sent shivers down her spine and made her knees so weak she longed to nestle against his strong body, to feel his arms . . .

The ringing of the phone broke the spell and she gasped as he cursed and turned to answer it. By the time she caught her breath, it was clear that the business call was going to take some time, so she gave him a quick wave and stepped outside—away from temptation.

A walk on the beach, that's what she needed. A chance to clear her head and make some sense of the emotions that seemed to ambush her whenever she was alone with Trevor. And to figure out if she'd just made a big mistake when she'd agreed to stay on a few more days.

Diana sighed. She'd always wondered what it would be like to behave impulsively, to follow her emotions as Eileen always had. Well, now she knew—it was as scary as her first ride on a roller coaster. And probably a lot more dangerous, yet how could she stop? Deep inside, she knew that she had no desire to turn back from whatever lay ahead. She couldn't if she was ever going to really get to know herself. Besides, she wanted the ride, the excitement, the final thrill of discovering the magic that had been missing from her marriage.

"Diana." His voice sent a shiver down her spine in spite of the warm sun that caressed her.

She was smiling when she turned to face him and he felt the jolt like an electric shock. Sheer delight made him laugh. She wasn't angry at the interruption as he'd feared. In fact, she looked happier than she'd been in the kitchen. "Where are you headed?" he asked, though he really didn't care.

She shrugged, her eyes glowing. "Any suggestions?"

Several occurred to him, but none of them involved walking, so he forced them back. From the few hints Crystal had dropped, he was beginning to suspect that Diana had been deeply hurt by her "ex" and he didn't want to rush her. "We could check out the meadow and see if the goats are any friendlier in daylight."

"As long as the sun's bright, the billy goat won't be able to sneak up on you."

"Good point." He caught her hand as they left the sand and headed across the rough grass toward the band of trees that separated his land from the meadows where the islanders grazed their goats. "Now let me tell you what else I have planned for tomorrow."

Diana leaned back in the padded booth of the restaurant with a sigh, her gaze on Trevor, enjoying the wonder of just watching him as he talked to Crystal. It was already late afternoon of the happiest day she could remember. Crystal was giggling and relaxed, acting like any normal daughter having fun on vacation with her family.

She caught her breath, straightening up as the implications of her thoughts swept through her. That was it, wasn't it? All day, she'd marveled at the fun they'd been having. First the easy camaraderie as Trevor showed them the lovely vistas of New Providence, then later his teasing acceptance of his role as package carrier during their tour of the shops and the endless temptations of the Nassau Straw Market. She'd thought it was the place, but being here had nothing to do with her happiness. It was sharing the day with Trevor and Crystal.

"So what do you think, Diana, are you up to a tour of the night spots tonight?" Trevor's question forced her attention back to the present.

"Oh, don't you think with an early-morning flight . . ."

"Don't be a drag, Diana. Say yes. We can sleep on the plane. We're talking fantastic resorts here, with real entertainment, and Trevor says he can get us into some of the shows if he calls right away." Crystal's animation seemed to ebb slightly as she faced Diana.

"It's been such a special day . . ." Trevor's pleading gaze melted her reservations.

Feeling caught in the middle, she gave in without a fight. "Whatever you two want to do is fine with me."

"Great, so which shows can we see?" Crystal turned her full attention back to Trevor.

Diana took a sip of lemonade, her earlier joy fading as she realized from Crystal's words that her niece still expected her to be flying back with her tomorrow, mostly because she hadn't remembered to tell Crystal about her change of plans. Or hadn't wanted to disturb their new closeness by telling her.

But would it? Would Crystal even care that she'd decided to stay behind? It worried her to realize how little she knew the girl she'd once considered a daughter. Had Crystal finally come to understand why Diana hadn't been able to stay with Ken, or was their new closeness just the result of her bringing Trevor into Crystal's life? Even the thought gave her a chill.

"Hey, don't look so grim, we're going to have fun tonight, I promise." Trevor's gentle touch on her cheek sent a tingle of electricity through Diana. "Now you two hold the fort while I go make a couple of calls and set everything up; then we'll head back to the guest house to get ready."

It took Diana several seconds to get her breathing back under control as Trevor slid out of the booth and disappeared into a dim hall. The man had a way of distracting her that was both delightful and a little frightening. She'd never felt such a mixture of power and vulnerability before. She had a strong hunch that it could be addicting.

"He's really fun, isn't he?" Crystal's sigh brought her attention back to the girl across the table.

Diana nodded. "Glad you came?"

Crystal giggled. "Jennifer is not going to believe any of this. And wait till she sees all the clothes. She's going to be green for a month. Trevor makes her mom's latest look like a real jerk."

Crystal's cynicism swept over her like a cold breeze, immediately bringing Diana to Trevor's defense. "It's not a contest, Crystal. Trevor really cares about you. His father cheated him out of the joy of raising his daughter just as he cheated you out of knowing your father."

"He wouldn't have had time for me, anyway. Haven't you seen that photo gallery he calls an office? He never gave Mom a thought, not after he met his perfect Amanda. I guess I'm just lucky she couldn't have kids; now he needs me."

Diana just stared at Crystal, too stunned by her bitter assessment of the situation to even protest.

"He's no different from you, you know. When you were right there at Cliffton, it was great; but once you decided you didn't want to be Mrs. Foster anymore, you were out of there without a backward glance. You didn't give a damn how I felt. Now you've found Trevor and, all of a sudden, I'm high on your list of people to care about again. But I guess it's like Jennifer says, that's just the way grown-ups operate, right?"

"Crystal, I never . . . I couldn't stay on at Cliffton. You know Ken made it impossible. I didn't have a job. But that didn't mean that my feelings toward you changed, I just . . ." The attack was so sudden, she found herself unable to fight back; it was all she could do to keep from crying.

How had she missed the anger? All this time Crystal had been furious and she'd thought . . . Diana swallowed hard. She hadn't thought, not really. In her misery and worry about Mom and trying to find a job and a new life, she'd mostly just felt sorry for herself and resented the way Crystal had turned away from her. But how could she explain . . .

She got no chance. Trevor was already on his way back across the busy restaurant, his wide smile making it clear that his phone calls had been successful. Crystal's enthusiastic welcome to him twisted the knife of jealousy in her already sore heart. Had she really lost Crystal's love and respect because of the divorce? Even thinking about it hurt.

"Hey, smile, Diana, this is supposed to be a fun evening. I know you like to dance, so what's the problem?" Trevor's question as they left the restaurant carried an edge of something more than idle teasing, and when she met his gaze, she could see the concern in his eyes.

Realizing that he probably thought her mood had to do with her initial disapproval of the nightclub tour and was worried that he'd made a mistake, she forced a smile. Her sorrow had nothing to do with him, so she didn't want to ruin this last evening of his first excursion into fatherhood. "I'm just trying to decide what to wear tonight. I didn't come prepared for such a glamorous evening."

The mention of clothes brought Crystal into the conversation and, within moments, they'd all slipped back into the teasing camaraderie that Diana had so enjoyed earlier. This time, however, her happiness was tempered by the realization that it was only an illusion. They weren't a family at all; in fact, as in much of her life these days, she seemed simply to be playing a part.

Diana gritted her teeth, then managed to laugh. If she was acting, she might as well give an Academy Award performance for Trevor's sake. And for her own. It frightened her a little to realize just how much she wanted to believe in the illusion they'd created.

By the time they drove back to the guest house through the silence of the waning night, Diana no longer cared whether it was reality or illusion. The night had been so perfect, she just wanted to treasure it. Trevor had not only managed to choose shows that kept them laughing, but he'd taken them to a club where there were plenty of other teenagers to distract Crystal—giving him and Diana a few moments of blissful privacy. They'd had a chance to snuggle close on the dance floor, to whisper a few words of encouragement to each other. She hated to see the evening end.

"Geeze, I don't want to go back tomorrow," Crystal moaned from the backseat. "Do you think you could call and tell them that the flight was canceled or something? Some of the kids I talked to said they were flying back Monday and they invited me to go out sailing with them tomorrow."

"There will be other vacations here," Trevor said before Diana could speak. "Besides, didn't you tell me you had a quiz on Monday?"

Crystal groaned. "I've been trying to forget. Now

I'll have to study on the plane. Will you help me, Diana? You were always good in algebra.''

Diana swallowed hard, suddenly realizing that she hadn't gotten around to telling Crystal that she wasn't going home with her. This was not the time she would have chosen. "I . . . ah . . . won't be on the plane with you, Crystal."

"You're staying?" Crystal's weary tone vanished, replaced by outrage. "Since when?"

"Well, I originally planned to see if I could get on your flight, but . . ." Diana closed her eyes, cursing her inability to speak out in her own defense. She'd never been so wishy-washy before; she'd always known exactly what she thought and felt and she'd expressed it firmly—until Ken came into her life.

"I asked Diana to stay over a couple of days." Trevor entered the conversation easily. "We need to talk about the financial arrangements and she knows how everything was set up before. Also, I want to go over the papers from Wilding that you brought with you." His voice softened. "We've been so busy having fun that I didn't get much chance to do that."

Crystal said nothing and the silence tightened around Diana like a noose. Guilt forced her to speak up. "Is there some reason you need for me to fly back with you, Crystal? If there is, I'll try to get on the flight tomorrow. I mean, Trevor and I can always settle the details by telephone . . ."

"No, no reason. I got myself out here alone, so I can get back to school on my own. I just assumed that you'd be heading home, that's all."

There wasn't a trace of emotion in Crystal's voice, but Diana felt the stinging anger anyway. She longed to reach out to her niece, but she knew instinctively that she'd be rebuffed. The chasm between them had grown too wide to be bridged by a few words or a hug. "I'll be back in a few days and then maybe we can plan a weekend together."

"Yeah, maybe." Crystal's lack of enthusiasm confirmed Diana's suspicions and destroyed the last of the evening's magic spell. Even Trevor's tender touch as he helped her from the car couldn't melt the ice that seemed to be forming inside her. She dared not put her trust in him or anyone else; there was too little of her left to risk.

Diana felt nothing except relief as she watched Crystal's plane take off the next morning, but when she turned to Trevor, his sorrow shamed her. She wanted to reach out to him, hold him close and assure him that he'd be seeing Crystal again soon, but she couldn't. Her very real vulnerability held her prisoner.

Suddenly, a grin replaced his grim look. "Hey, we did it!" His arms surrounded her with warmth and his touch lifted her spirits as he hugged her. "She really had fun, Diana. I think she's looking forward to spending more time with me."

"Of course she is. She had a wonderful time and so did I. You're going to be a terrific father, I told you that."

"I'm sure going to try, but I couldn't have done it without you. We're a great team, Diana."

"Yeah, terrific." She couldn't meet his gaze because she knew her face would show the doubts she was feeling. She didn't want to dampen his happiness, so she decided to change the subject. She really didn't want to talk about Crystal until she'd had a chance to get some perspective on her own troubled relationship with her. "So what do we do now?"

"Well, we could go back to the guest house and just laze around until time for the interisland flight." He spoke softly, his tone almost a caress. "Unless there's somewhere else you'd like to go?"

For a heartbeat, her doubts held her prisoner; then she shook them off and lifted her gaze to meet his. "Sounds good to me," she whispered, wondering if he could hear the wild pounding of her heart as he took her hand.

As he drove along the narrow back road that led from the inland airport to the stretch of beach where Floyd McMurtry had built his mansion and the charming guest house, Trevor felt his euphoria slipping away. He could tell that something was bugging Diana and had been since yesterday afternoon. She tried to hide her feelings, but whenever her guard was down for even a moment, he could see the sadness in her face.

Should he ignore it, maybe try to make her forget . . . The scenarios for diverting her attention that his mind supplied made him catch his breath, but he forced the erotic fantasies away. There'd been a time when he was sure passion could cure all ills, but he'd outgrown that illusion. And what he and Diana had just shared was far too special to be risked for a few hours of wild lovemaking. At least, he hoped it was.

He took a deep breath and plunged in before he could change his mind and follow his lustier instincts. "Is something wrong between you and Crystal, Diana?"

Diana gulped in shock at the question, then realized that she should have expected it. She'd already seen how sensitive Trevor could be, so why hadn't she realized that he would notice her moods as well as his daughter's?

"I just realized yesterday that I hurt Crystal badly when I left Cliffton last spring. She still hasn't forgiven me." She tried for honesty, though she was far from ready to talk to him about the end of her marriage.

"Forgiven you for what? Quitting your job?"

"I was forced to leave. My . . . my ex-husband was, still is, head of the school. When our marriage ended, he refused to have me on the grounds, let alone teaching there." Her voice cracked a little as the ugly memories swept through her. "I thought Crystal understood, but I was wrong."

"You were fired?" Trevor fought down a surge of

pure fury. Now he understood the pain he'd heard in her voice when she mentioned her job at the school. He also had to revise his image of her ex-husband from that of an insensitive jock to the kind of man who would be running an exclusive boarding school for young ladies.

"My contract was not renewed. That was the way Ken termed it; but yes, basically, I was fired." Bitterness washed through her, but she stopped herself before she added the words that Ken had flung at her when he told her what she could expect if she insisted upon leaving him. "I'll see to it that the whole world knows that you're a washout as a wife and a teacher."

Another jolt of anger hit him as he realized what she hadn't said. It was obvious to him that she'd been shut out of getting another job by the bastard who'd hurt her. He didn't need to hear the words to know how gossip could be used against someone as young and lovely as Diana. He had to force himself to ease his grip on the steering wheel before he left dents in it. He tried to focus on the problem before he said more than he should about the man.

"So why does Crystal blame you?"

Diana shrugged. "Because I'm not there for her and Ken probably is. He's very good at charming young girls, making them feel special and important. It's what makes him so good at his job. He wins their friendship and respect and that keeps the school running smoothly."

"He wouldn't hurt her?" The surge of protective anger nearly choked him.

Suddenly aware of the tension that seemed to radiate from Trevor's body, Diana forced her own anger away so she could reassure him. "No, I'm sure he wouldn't. He was always good to her; even at the end, he did everything he could to keep our breakup from hurting Crystal."

"What about after you left?"

She swallowed a sigh, realizing that she wasn't going to be able to leave out anything. Because Crystal was involved, Trevor had a right to the facts. "If anything, I think her anger comes from his lack of attention to her. You see, I didn't realize it before, but I think Crystal was seeing Ken as a father figure. She's angry at me not only because I'm not there, but because she's lost her illusion of having a family like everyone else."

"She doesn't need an illusion or a substitute for a father, she has me."

Diana winced, aware that her words had hurt and angered him. She found herself wishing that she'd gotten on the plane with Crystal after all. It seemed she had a better chance of coming to an understanding with her niece than she did of keeping on the good side of Trevor Sinclair. Or was that just another illusion?

Smooth move, Sinclair, Trevor mocked himself. *Diana needs cheering up and you give her the heavy father routine.* But what could he do—offer to hire someone to break old Ken's kneecaps? It shocked him to discover just how appealing that sounded. Maybe looking like a pirate was having more of an effect than he'd realized. Or maybe it was something else.

Unwilling to even consider the possibility that he was getting too involved with Diana, he forced his brain into action. "What do you say we take a swim, then pack up and go out for a leisurely lunch before our flight?"

"That sounds perfect." Diana faced him, suddenly wanting him to see the gratitude in her face. "And you're right, Trevor, Crystal doesn't need any other father figure. I'm sure she's feeling much better about everything now."

Trevor caught her hand and lifted her fingers to his lips, touching them gently. "I hope we all are, Diana."

A shiver chased through her at his touch, but the sudden appearance of a truck coming at them along the narrow track forced him to drop her hand and concentrate on his driving, ending the moment. Still, she kept remembering that special feeling through the rest of their time on New Providence Island and drawing courage from it, as well as hope.

It was late afternoon when the nearly empty inter-island plane settled on the landing strip at Bellington Cay. "Where is everyone?" Diana asked, remembering the crowd that had been waiting there when Crystal arrived.

"This is Sunday. The rush usually starts mid-week or later unless it's a holiday." Trevor collected their suitcases and headed for his car, which waited in nearly solitary splendor.

"Then there are probably empty rooms at the resorts," she murmured, remembering the lack of lodging that had greeted her harried arrival, what now seemed a lifetime ago.

Trevor stopped so suddenly she nearly stumbled into him. He turned to face her, his eyes narrowed. "What are you thinking?"

A shiver traced down her spine at the anger in his eyes. "Just that maybe I should . . . I mean, for propriety's sake maybe it would look better if I . . ." Her inability to finish a sentence told her that his gaze was having a serious impact on her thought processes.

"No!" His own vehemence startled him.

"But . . ."

"Don't run away from me, Diana. We've come too far, gotten too close for you to be afraid. Besides, we have so much to discuss, so many decisions to make." He stopped speaking, well aware that he couldn't force her to stay in his house, yet desperate to keep her at his side.

"I just didn't want to cause any gossip." When he looked at her like that, she didn't want to go anywhere except with him—a fact that turned on her warning voice, which she managed to ignore.

"Everyone knows that you're family, so there won't

be any gossip." Trevor set down the suitcases and reached out to brush back a tawny curl that had blown across her cheek. "I'd never ask you to do anything that would make you uncomfortable, Diana. Or cause you any pain. Don't you know that by now?"

The heat of his fingers moved through her like a river of lava, causing her pulse to race and making it difficult to breathe. The honest concern in his gaze melted all her defenses, making it impossible for her to escape the danger of being alone with him—a danger that came not from him, but from within her.

"Will you stay with me?" His fingers moved slowly along the line of her jaw to her chin; then his thumb brushed gently over her lower lip. "Please."

"Of course I will." The words came on the crest of a sigh of longing that she couldn't keep inside. The shivers of wanting that shook her body made it clear no other answer was possible.

"Good, then let's get home. I'm anxious to see if Harlan has come up with anything on Wilding."

"What do you mean?" The shift of subjects left her a little dizzy. Or was it the sensations that continued to sizzle through her even after he'd stepped back and picked up the suitcases again?

"I asked him to do some digging, make sure that what they offer is the best for Crystal. Now that I know about her, there are no limits. If she can get a better musical education in Europe or in a different school in the U.S., that's what I want for her."

"Europe?" She could barely say the word. "But that's so far away, Trevor. You can't send her to Europe. She's just seventeen and . . ." Horror kept her from going on. Never in her wildest dreams had she even considered that he might suggest something so awful.

"She deserves the best, Diana. You told me that yourself. If that means studying abroad, then I think she should have her chance." He closed the trunk and turned to face her, his gaze challenging. "Don't you?"

Protests crowded her throat, but she kept her lips pressed together, fighting the urge to scream at him. Her mother's words echoed through her mind mockingly. Was he doing it? Was he already planning ways to take Crystal away from them?

"Diana? What is it?" The concern in his face broke through her panic, scattering her doubts and helping her to regain some of her composure.

"I just never thought of her going so far away. I even hated having her alone at Cliffton this year. She needs family and love, Trevor, not banishment to a foreign country." Her voice broke at the thought of Crystal alone in some distant land. She had to bite her lip to keep from crying.

"If that's what she needs, that's what she'll have, Diana. I would never send her away, unless that was what she wanted. Can't you trust me? Don't you know by now that I just want Crystal to be happy?" Trevor watched the myriad emotions that crossed Diana's lovely face and his momentary anger and hurt faded as quickly as they had come.

She was afraid, he realized, afraid of losing Crystal. Without thinking further, he pulled her close, appalled to feel the tremors that were shaking her body. Dear Lord, what had her ex-husband done to undermine her confidence so completely? And how could he make up for all that she'd suffered and bring back the sparkling spirit of adventure she'd exhibited so often when they first met?

Diana closed her eyes, surrendering to the delicious wonder of having her cheek pressed against his chest, his intoxicating scent filling her nostrils. She could hear the strong beat of his heart, sense when it accelerated to match the pounding of her own. Her doubts and fears fled, vanquished by the potent ache of longing for a different embrace. She didn't want his comfort. She wanted . . . She wanted him!

EIGHT

Diana considered her startling realization throughout the drive from the airstrip to Trevor's house. Could she be falling in love? That was something she'd vowed never to do again after she'd fled the shambles of her marriage. But what else could the tidal waves of emotion mean? Or more important, what was she going to do about them?

Her initial fantasies did nothing to calm her passionate longing, and the sense of coming home that swept over her when Trevor parked in front of the house only added to the illusion. For that had to be what it was, she told herself, just an illusion born of her loneliness and frustration and nurtured by Trevor's tenderness and devastating appeal. After all, what woman wouldn't be attracted to such a gorgeous man?

That thought did nothing to ease the butterflies dancing in her stomach. She didn't want to think of other women in Trevor's arms, not when she remembered how strong they were and how tenderly he'd held her. And when he'd kissed her . . . She swallowed hard. That was something she'd better not even think about.

"You ready to go inside?" Trevor's teasing question forced her back to reality.

She picked up her totebag, purse, and the two big bags that contained the results of yesterday's Christmas shopping spree at the straw market. This mooning over Trevor had to stop. She'd come back to Bellington Cay for one purpose only—to secure Crystal's future education. Anything that distracted her from that goal . . .

Her sense of humor suddenly bubbled through the doubts and fears and she barely managed to control a highly unsuitable giggle. What she'd been feeling was a whole lot more than just distracted! And she wasn't exactly sure she wanted to ignore the feelings, even supposing she could.

"It's nice to see you smiling." Trevor interrupted her reverie again.

Diana looked into his eyes and knew immediately that she'd come back here for her own sake as well as to make sure things went smoothly for Crystal. Heart pounding, she decided to trust her instincts and Trevor. "Being here with you makes me feel like smiling."

Her simple confession hit him like a lightning bolt, drying his mouth and making him ache with longing. If he'd had any doubts about her effect on him, they were swept away by the heat that pulsed through him. He definitely wanted her with every hungry inch of his body. The question was—what was he going to do about it?

Had she been any other woman, he wouldn't have hesitated to seduce her; but this was Eileen's sister, Crystal's aunt. Making love with her could have consequences far beyond the ecstacy her tempting body promised. But how could he deny the fires that were blazing between them?

Before he had to answer his own question, the front door opened and Louise came out. "You have a call, Trevor. It's Harlan Cole."

Diana let her breath out slowly, startled to realize that she'd been holding it. The man definitely lit her fire, no question about that. She grinned sheepishly at

Louise as the housekeeper took one of the bulky sacks. "I did my Christmas shopping and now I'm wondering how I'm going to get all this home on the plane."

"Trevor can have them shipped for you, don't worry." Louise led the way inside, then asked, "So did you have a good time in Nassau?" There was no sign of disapproval in her gaze or tone, just the friendliness that Diana had enjoyed from her first full day on the island.

Laughing at her own foolish fears, she launched herself on a carefully edited description of their stay on New Providence Island. It was like talking to an old friend and reminded her forcefully of just how lonely she'd been since she'd left Cliffton and all her friends there. The emotional cost of her divorce had been high and her sense of isolation since very real, which probably explained why her self-esteem had been so battered and why she still had so many doubts about her decisions.

But that was going to change. Coming here had been the right thing to do, despite Mom's dire predictions. And meeting Trevor had brought something new and exciting into her life, reviving feelings she'd assumed were destroyed forever. Whatever the future might hold, she meant to put aside her doubts and explore those feelings.

Trevor sat in his office for several minutes after he hung up the phone. Amanda smiled at him from every side, but he scarcely saw the photos that had once haunted him. He was too busy wondering just how he should take Harlan's final words of warning. They'd come right after Trevor finished describing their rewarding time in Nassau.

"She sounds like an exciting woman, Trev, but you be careful. I checked around some and the word is that she really damaged her husband's career. Ken Foster is a good fifteen years older than she and very respected in academic circles. He'd lost his wife in an accident about four years before he took over at Cliffton School. She evidently swept him off his feet and into marriage, then got bored and wanted out. That's a conservative school, so they were upset enough about a marriage within the academic family, then to have it come apart after a year . . .''

Disturbed by what Harlan seemed to be hinting, Trevor had leaped to Diana's defense. ''I doubt that you got the whole story. From what I've seen, she was pretty battered by the divorce and I know how much it's cost her emotionally.''

''I'm not making any judgments, man, just offering some facts for your consideration. That's what you pay me for. But more than that, I'm your friend and I know how miserable you've been since you lost Amanda. I just want you to keep your eyes open.''

Trevor had forced a chuckle past the lump of anger in his throat and kept his temper by reminding himself that Harlan hadn't met Diana and that he was his best friend. ''She's Crystal's aunt, Harlan, so I'm not going to do anything stupid. There's too much at stake.''

''Okay, then I hope you have a ball. You're already sounding better. Being a dad must agree with you.''

''I could get to like it real well.''

Trevor sighed, then stared out at the restless sea. That was the truth all right. He did love the emotions he'd felt just being around Crystal, but honesty made him admit that Diana had been a large part of everything. Just being around her, laughing with her, having her to talk to when things got rough with Crystal, holding her . . .

He got to his feet with a curse. Thinking about Harlan's warning was getting him nowhere. He needed action. He needed to spend some more time with Diana. Once they settled the details of Crystal's future education, they'd have plenty of time to explore the attraction that seemed to be growing between them. He pointedly ignored the small voice in his head that informed him that spending time with Diana was exactly what was causing his confusion.

He followed the sound of feminine laughter to the kitchen, then joined Diana and Louise at the table, where they were sipping lemonade and eating cookies. His uneasiness disappeared as they talked about the weekend, and his sense of satisfaction grew as he watched the pleasure in Diana's face as he told her what Harlan had said about the Wilding School of Music.

"Then you'll make the arrangements so she can start school there next fall?" The relief in her voice made it clear just how worried she'd been about his suggestion that he might send Crystal to Europe to study.

"We can call her tonight, if you like. Make her feel better about having to return to the snow and cold." He found just basking in the glow of Diana's smile surprisingly rewarding.

"So do you want me to fix something special for dinner tonight?" Louise asked, breaking into his thoughts.

Trevor studied Diana, a fascinating new idea taking form in his mind. "I was thinking more about taking a picnic dinner up the beach a ways, maybe eating while we watch the sunset. How does that sound, Diana?"

The cookie turned to sawdust on her tongue, clogging her throat so that she couldn't even breathe—or maybe it was the smoldering heat of his gaze that paralyzed her. Images of their last visit to Hibiscus Cove filled her mind and sent a wave of heat through her.

"Diana?" Trevor's tone changed to one of concern. "We don't have to, if you're not in the mood for a picnic. I just thought . . ."

He didn't have to tell her what he thought; she'd read it in his gaze and felt it deep inside. She washed the cookie down with a sip of lemonade and pressed the cool glass against her flushed cheek. "That sounds like a marvelous idea, just perfect. How about turkey sandwiches and some of the other leftovers from Thanksgiving? I always think it all tastes better after the holiday, mostly because I eat too much at the dinner.''

She had a feeling she wasn't making a whole lot of sense, but she had to say something to break the sensual silence that blazed between them. After all, it wouldn't do for Louise to guess what Trevor had in mind for . . .

Diana straightened in her chair. There was nothing for Louise to guess about, because there was nothing going on between them. Nothing except friendship and caring and their shared interest in Crystal. And an attraction hot enough to give off sparks in a blizzard.

''I'll help you get the stuff together,'' Louise said, getting to her feet at once. ''I've got some time before . . .''

''I can make sandwiches and pack a picnic basket,'' Diana interrupted, feeling a strong need for action and distraction. ''And I'm sure you could use a little extra time to prepare for your church program tonight.''

Within moments, she and Trevor were alone in the kitchen. Though the room had seemed cool earlier, now the lowering sun's rays were roasting. Or was it just because he was standing so close? Feeling appallingly like a girl in the throes of her first crush, Diana forced herself to move away from him to the refrigerator. ''So what shall we take?''

Since her nervousness made it clear that a trip up to his bedroom wasn't one of the options she had in mind, Trevor went to get the picnic basket and set it out on the table, hoping the activity would stimulate his brain to produce something more than erotic fantasies. Luckily, the sight of bread, turkey, and all the fixings did remind him that he was hungry for more than Diana's luscious lips, so he managed to make himself useful.

As they stepped out of the house, he found himself recalling the evening, less than two weeks ago, when he'd fled the house for a run on the beach and discovered a whole new life—a life that now seemed full of spectacular possibilities. Feeling younger than he had in years, he smiled down at Diana.

"You're in a good mood."

"I was just thinking how much my life has changed since the night we met. Everything seemed very empty and hopeless then and now . . ." He stopped himself, unwilling to reveal how deeply he felt about her entrance into his life.

"Now you have a daughter." Diana finished for him, sensing a subtle change in his mood. Had she misread his signals? Was she only seeing what she wanted to see when it came to Trevor? Or was she projecting her own feelings onto a man who might only be using her as an antidote to his grief?

"And your company." He shifted the heavy basket to his other hand and slipped an arm around her shoulders. "Having you here has been wonderful, Diana. You make me feel whole again and ready to take on the world and I'm grateful."

The honest feeling in his voice touched her and she stopped, facing him. "That goes both ways, Trevor. I guess you know from what I've told you that my life has been messed up for a while, too. Coming here, getting to know you has helped me put a lot of ugly memories behind me. I'm actually beginning to believe that I can have a real life again."

"Of course you can. You're a bright and beautiful woman. Don't let one man's cruelty turn you against life and love. You deserve so much happiness . . ." He let it trail off, disturbed by the growing intensity of his feelings. He hadn't meant to get so serious, not tonight. This was a time for easy laughter and gentle exploration and a whole lot of caution.

But caution was the last thing on his mind as they moved on along the deserted beach, his arm still around her shoulders, her body brushing close to his with every step they took. He'd been strong and caring and responsible through all the dark months of Amanda's suffering, and when he'd lost her, he'd thought his life was over, too, but now . . . Now he felt young and alive and very much aware of Diana's intoxicating closeness.

"Are we going to Hibiscus Cove?" Her voice was low, almost a whisper.

"The view of the sunset is incredible from there."

"Sunset." She was trembling, and he could feel it as he pressed her closer to his side.

"About an hour from now. Those clouds on the horizon will make it spectacular, you'll see." He scarcely knew what he was saying, and when she looked up at him, he understood that it didn't matter. Awareness and acceptance smoldered in her dark blue eyes. His body tightened in response and he wondered if he could bear the wait until dark.

Meeting his gaze made her knees so weak she doubted that she'd be able to make the long walk to the cove. *Lighten up,* she counseled herself, trying hard to think of a new subject, something that would counteract the almost visible electricity between them. "So . . . ah . . . what did Mr. Cole tell you about Wilding? Are there special classes for new students? Will Crystal have to take placement tests for her musical skills? Will I need to take her to the school for interviews?"

Trevor frowned at the sudden barrage of questions, resenting the change of subject until he caught the flicker of wariness in Diana's eyes. So she'd been feeling the heat as much as he had. That pleased him so much he happily recited every fact Harlan had told him about Wilding. It made the long walk pass quite quickly and eased away some of the singing tension that crackled between them.

The cove welcomed them with a serene loveliness that soothed the spirit even as the deserted stretch of sand teased her with its promise of privacy. This time Trevor led her beyond the powdery sand to a spot where the rocks guarded a grassy bower from the rhythmic waves that splashed against them. "The view should be perfect from here," he said, looking only into her eyes. "We can watch the colors without being blinded."

Her heart stopped for a moment, then bounced into aerobic speed as her breath caught in her throat. She nodded, unable to speak. Not that he seemed to expect her to say anything. His smile caressed her as he set the basket down and took her hands. The lowering sun bathed him in red-gold light, casting dramatic shadows across his lean features so that she was reminded again of his buccaneer appeal.

Was he going to ravish her here on this beach? The idea did nothing to slow her heart rate and a quiver of anticipation began deep inside her, spreading over her whole body so that she felt the weight of his gaze like a tangible caress. Was that, perhaps, what she really wanted from him?

Her inner voice cried out that she shouldn't even think such things, but she tuned it out. The old, timid Diana had always listened to that warning voice and obeyed it; but that Diana had died, been crushed by the ending of her supposedly perfect marriage. The person who'd come to Bellington Cay to pursue Crystal's dream was strong and adventurous, perhaps even strong enough to pursue a dream of her own.

"Well, I guess we'd better spread the blanket." Trevor's voice sounded slightly hoarse, but he welcomed her help with a grin as he shook out the blanket and covered the thick grass.

They were like characters in a play, Diana decided, as she sank down on the blanket and began taking the food from the basket. They carried on what sounded like a normal conversation, but she sensed that he was no more interested in her description of her mother's shop than she was in the details of the merger that Harlan had called him about. The real contact between them came each time their fingers touched or their eyes met and it had nothing to do with business.

They finished the food just as the sun began its final fiery plunge through the burning clouds. Trevor poured sparkling wine into two glasses and handed her one. "To a perfect sunset and the night it heralds."

Her mouth went dry as she touched her glass to his. There was no mistaking the desire in his eyes, the hunger that reached out to her and reminded her of her own deep longing to be in his arms. She nearly choked on the wine, having momentarily lost the ability to even swallow. He pulled her close against his side as they watched, mesmerized while the sun flamed its last and slipped beneath the darkness of the sea.

Night came so fast it stunned her. One moment the light spilled around them, the next darkness had erased the world, leaving them cradled in their shadowy nest with only the early stars above them. The quivering inside her intensified as she drained her wine and carefully set the empty glass in the basket.

Run, the voice inside her warned. *Don't make another mistake.* But she closed her mind to doubt and focused instead on Trevor. Shyly, she lifted a hand to touch his cheek, marveling at the softness of his beard as she explored the contours of his face beneath it.

When she reached his mouth, his lips caught at her fingers, drawing one inside for a moment. The quivering became a full-blown shiver as his tongue caressed her finger, hinting at the sensual wonders ahead. She offered no argument when he freed her finger and took her willing lips instead. The thick locks of his midnight hair offered another avenue of exploration for her questing fingers as she tried to memorize every inch of his head and neck, his shoulders and back even as he plundered the depths of her mouth.

Trevor slipped a hand beneath the back of her loose cotton top, caressing the bare skin above the waistband of her shorts. His hot fingers left a trail of delight as they moved over her, heating each spot he touched as he sought the softness of her breast. A throbbing need swept through her as his hand gently cradled her swollen flesh and she moaned under the continuing magic of his kiss.

"Diana." His voice was a growl of need as he nibbled kisses down the side of her neck, then turned his head so he could press his mouth against the pounding pulse at the base of her throat. She shivered again as his tongue measured the rate of her racing heart.

Shaken by the exquisite sensations that came from his light stroking of her taut nipple, Diana nipped at his ear. She rubbed against his hand, luxuriating in the feel of his slightly rough skin against her. Then she ran her tongue along the side of his neck, tasting the salty musk of his skin, memorizing his special flavor.

"I want to see you." His fingers were on the buttons of her shirt, but he made no move to open them until she nodded. As he freed them, she put her own trembling hands to work unbuttoning his shirt, then gasped as she buried her fingers in the dark curls that covered his broad chest. She pressed her palm against his chest, excited to feel the wild pounding of his heart as it echoed her own.

His lips followed the path of his fingers as he opened her shirt, each kiss igniting another curl of flame within her. Once her shirt was open, he released her lacy bra, freeing one aching breast to his hungry mouth. A shudder took Diana's breath away and with it the last of the restraints and barricades she'd erected to protect herself.

"Oh, Trevor, Trevor," she gasped as she slipped her hands beneath his shirt, digging her nails into his muscular shoulders, trying desperately to hold on as her familiar world spun out of control.

"I won't hurt you." His whisper was labored as he lifted his head and met her gaze. "I swear it, Diana."

For a moment she teetered on the edge; then she answered from her heart. "I trust you, Trevor."

His touch was incredibly gentle as he eased off her shirt, then her bra. "You are so lovely." He shrugged out of his shirt, then pulled her close as his lips found hers again.

Shivers of delight spread through her as his tickling curls touched her sensitive breasts. She rubbed against him, wanting to purr like a cat, luxuriating in the sensations that burned through her. It was heavenly, but not enough. She wanted . . . needed much, much more.

"I want you." Trevor's moan as his hand slid caressingly over her quivering stomach echoed her own needs perfectly.

Unable to form the words, she arched against his hand, inviting his exploration, offering her willing body. His touch was sure and practiced as he accepted her invitation. Her shorts and panties were banished as he devoured her with kisses that produced more heat than the blazing noonday sun. Never had she felt such passion, such loving hunger as when he sought out the secret places of her body and brought them to life.

His touch was magic, weaving a spell over her, awakening a hunger she'd never known before. Driven by her own need, she answered his caresses, his kisses, making her own passionate demands, so that he, too, was soon moaning for more. As their bodies joined at last, she clung to him with a fierceness that carried her to the brink of madness and into the golden pool of dreams on the other side.

Trevor cradled Diana's soft body tight against his own, turning carefully to ease his weight from her, yet trying to keep their bodies fused as the cooling night air dried the dampness of love from their skin. At the moment he was too stunned to even think; he could only feel the final shudders of completion as they eased the tension from his body.

Diana sighed, her breath stirring the hair on his chest as her long legs tightened around him slightly, as though she, too, wanted the moment of oneness to last forever. He shifted slightly so that he could kiss her forehead, burying his nose in the softness of her hair, drinking in her scent until he was dizzy with it. If only they could stay this way forever . . .

Forever? The word seemed to swell in his head, demanding his attention when all he wanted to do was stroke Diana's soft skin and lose himself in the sensation. He didn't want to think about tomorrow or the consequences of what they'd just done. He just wanted . . .

"Trevor." Diana's voice broke through the drifting fog that seemed to surround them. "I think maybe we should be getting back to the house."

"But it's so nice here." He kept his eyes closed against the encroachment of reality as he kissed the tender skin below her ear. "So nice holding you."

"I'm afraid it won't be for long." Her tone seemed more amused than passionate.

Disturbed, Trevor opened his eyes, then blinked, unable to believe what he was seeing. The fog seemed to have escaped from his mind and now surrounded them. He gulped as the cold, wet breeze stirred the fog and sent shivers over his rapidly cooling body. "I see what you mean, but I sure hate to move." He hugged her even closer, aware that she was shivering, too.

"We could always continue in front of a nice roaring fire," Diana suggested as she nibbled lightly at the skin on his shoulder.

"That is definitely an offer I can't refuse." Trevor relinquished his embrace reluctantly, feeling even colder as she moved away to pull on her clothes.

Within moments, they'd dressed and packed away the remains of their picnic. Then, wrapped snugly together in the cocoon of the blanket, they made their way along the barely visible beach, reaching the house just as the first drops of rain came spattering down and the wind began to shred the fog.

Light spilled around them as Diana dropped the blanket and shook back her hair, suddenly conscious of how she must look. Not that it seemed to matter, since Trevor didn't even glance in her direction. "I'll go get that fire started," he murmured, dropping the picnic basket on the kitchen table as he headed through the door to the living room.

Was he ashamed to face her now? Diana shivered, though the kitchen was warm enough. Was he sorry for what they'd done—for making love to her? A sob rose in her throat at the thought and she stepped quickly into the small bath that was located near the back door for the convenience of swimmers.

Her reflection in the mirror stunned her. Her lips were swollen from his kisses and her hair a tangled mess, but her skin seemed to glow. She looked like a woman who'd just made love. A shiver moved through her as she realized that was exactly how she felt, too. But what did Trevor feel?

Sounds from outside the door told her that Trevor was now fixing the coffee maker. She stayed where she was, unwilling to let him see how vulnerable his touch had made her.

Trevor's voice broke into her moment of anxiety. "Diana, I'm going up to change. Do you still want to call Crystal tonight?"

She glanced at her watch, startled to realize that it would still be reasonably early in Sutton Falls. She swallowed hard, not sure she could talk to Crystal or anyone else just now. Yet how could she refuse? "Sure," she called. "But I'll go up and change first, too."

Something was wrong. Trevor frowned as he climbed the stairs. Diana wasn't the type to hide in the bathroom. At least, he didn't think she was. Suddenly all the magical closeness they'd shared seemed to ebb as he realized that there was no way he could know how Diana would react.

The truth was, they'd met less than two weeks ago,

were really almost strangers; yet they'd shared so much living here together, planning for Crystal's visit, then making it work. And more than that, there was what they'd shared on the beach tonight, he reminded himself, carefully keeping his eyes averted from the framed picture of Amanda that sat on his dresser.

Had it just been sex? When he'd held her afterward, he'd been sure that it was far more, but now . . . now the doubts were coming back. The few times he'd tried to find release in the arms of a woman after Amanda's death had left him empty and aching, but tonight he'd felt renewed and full of hope. At least he had until they reached the house and Diana disappeared into the bathroom without a word. A chill touched him. What if he'd messed everything up because he couldn't keep his hands off her?

By the time Diana went back downstairs, she was feeling much better. She'd come to terms with what had happened between them, put it into perspective— well, sort of. At least, she'd done her best to protect her vulnerable heart with rationalizations even as she was donning her favorite deep rose velour jogging suit, the one that protected her body from icy winds and prying eyes.

"You look . . . warm." Trevor's words came with a grin that made her feel much warmer—all over.

Diana swallowed hard, keeping back the words that she felt it was much too soon to say. Instead, she managed a smile of her own. "So, are you ready to give Crystal the good news about Wilding?"

"How about we both do it? I can place the call from my office; then you can talk down here. I'm sure she'll have plenty to say to both of us."

"No doubt." A knot tightened in her stomach, but she ignored it. What had just happened between her and Trevor had nothing to do with Crystal, so there was no reason to be feeling guilty or nervous.

"Coffee first? Or will that make it too late to call?"

"Let's not take a chance. You told me yourself how slow the overseas operators can be." She definitely wanted to get the call over before she spent any more time close to Trevor—if he even wanted to be close to her again.

"Do you have the number?"

"Why don't I place the call while you're on your way up? Maybe we'll be lucky and get right through." Diana met his gaze and felt the shock clear to her toes. Though she'd meant to go right to the kitchen, her feet seemed to have taken root where she was. He had no right to look so appealing and sexy and she shouldn't be thinking of the way his hands felt on her bare skin, the way his lips . . .

He bent his head, touching his lips to hers for just a heartbeat. "I already feel incredibly lucky tonight," he whispered, then turned and ran up the stairs without a backward glance.

NINE

The call had gone better than she'd dared hope. Once Crystal heard the news, she'd been so excited, she'd never asked anything about what had happened after her plane took off. In fact, Diana realized as she poured coffee into the mugs Trevor had set out, that she hadn't even asked Diana when she planned to come home.

That was a question she had better consider, she reminded herself. Now that Crystal's future was back on track, she needed to tend to her own. After she made peace with Mom, of course, a thought that did nothing to ease the nervous flutter that started in her stomach the moment she heard Trevor coming down the metal stairs.

His happy smile melted her heart and destroyed all her good intentions about leaving here as soon as possible. "Did you hear how happy she sounded? And she actually thanked me for arranging everything so quickly." He leaned against the door frame and some of the pleasure began ebbing from his expression. "Do you think she'll ever be able to . . . ah . . . call me Dad?"

"Give her time, Trevor. This is all pretty new. She's never had a dad, just a father whose name was synony-

mous with betrayal and desertion. Once she starts thinking of you as her father, the rest will follow naturally.''
She handed him his coffee, then followed him across
the living room to the couch he'd drawn up close to
the fireplace.

Trevor hesitated, wanting to sit on the couch with
her but not sure of his welcome. The moment she'd
appeared in the very high-necked and loose-fitting jogging suit, he'd known that she was pulling back from
what they'd shared on the beach. What he wasn't sure
about was why.

She'd held nothing back when they made love, so
why the barriers now? Did she want something he
hadn't offered her? But what? It was too soon for promises, wasn't it? After all, in many ways, they were still
strangers. Yet when he looked at her, the fire inside
him made that a lie.

Diana squirmed a little as Trevor finally stopped staring at her and sank down on the other end of the couch.
It was obvious that he was as uncomfortable as she,
which surprised her until she remembered that he'd
been married for much of his adult life. Happily married, she reminded herself firmly, suddenly sure that
he'd never cheated on his adored Amanda.

Was he feeling guilty now? That thought hadn't occurred to her before; but in a way, she realized that it
made sense. He was far from the young man who'd so
easily forgotten his love affair with Eileen; who'd
moved on and never looked back once he found the
right woman. Just imagining how deeply and completely he'd loved Amanda brought a pang of something
that felt very much like jealousy and shamed her.

Knowing that she was making herself crazy, she
forced her mind onto another track. ''So what else do
we need to decide for Crystal?''

A slight frown touched his forehead, then vanished
as he gave her a rather distracted look. ''I guess the

next thing would be deciding how she should spend her Christmas vacation.''

"Christmas?'' A hollow formed beneath her ribs.

"Well, while she was here, Crystal did mention that your mother would be staying in Arizona until spring, so I assumed that you probably hadn't made any specific plans for the holidays.''

"We really haven't had much time to even think about it,'' Diana admitted, remembering just how uninterested in Christmas she'd felt recently, especially when she thought about last year.

Last Christmas had been one of the few happy times in her marriage, mostly because it had been Ken's gift to her. He'd insisted on having a family Christmas, with her mother and Crystal staying with them throughout the holidays.

With Mom and Crystal at her side and Ken's instructions echoing in her ears, she'd prepared parties for the few staff, faculty, and students who'd remained at Cliffton. She spent the season spreading good cheer and playing the proper wife to the hilt. It was only afterward, when everyone was gone and Ken's decorations were packed away, that she realized there was nothing behind the illusion she'd worked so hard to create.

"Was there something special you wanted to do this year?'' Trevor's question pulled her back from the chasm of her dark memories.

"I just assumed that we'd go to Phoenix. The doctor said Mom shouldn't be in the cold, but I know she won't want to spend the holidays without us.''

"Is that what Crystal wants to do?''

"I don't know.'' The hollowness was now beginning to turn chilly. What was Trevor getting at? Did he mean to take Crystal somewhere else? Was he planning on introducing her to his friends and family, maybe shutting her real family out entirely? Her chill came from the suspicion that Crystal might welcome any offer he made, just to postpone the real confrontation that both

Crystal and Diana had been avoiding since the day Diana had told her niece about the divorce.

Trevor leaned forward, oblivious to her distress. "She really seemed sorry to be leaving here, don't you think? And she was just beginning to make friends with some of the island teenagers. Besides, according to Louise, there's always a great party going on here during the holidays. She claims the whole island celebrates in style."

Diana felt his gaze, but she couldn't meet it. She had no doubt that Crystal would jump at the chance to come back here and stay with Trevor. But where would that leave her? How could she face Mom or herself if they lost Crystal to Trevor's rich and powerful family?

What was the matter with her? Trevor felt a chill in spite of the heat of the fire he'd built. Diana looked so miserable he ached to pull her into his arms and kiss her until everything faded but the magic they'd shared on the beach. But what if that was the trouble? He didn't want to make things worse. He straightened up; he'd had enough of doubts and questions.

"What's wrong, Diana? You seem so troubled. Don't you want to spend Christmas here?"

"Me?" Her eyes widened and he could see the flickering of doubt and hope in their depths.

"Well, of course, you. You didn't think I meant to keep Crystal away from you, did you? I know how lonely Christmas can be when you have no one around that you care about; I wouldn't do that to you or to your mother, if you think she'd be willing to come here, too." He found it wonderfully easy to take her hands and draw her gently into his arms.

His words and the loving kindness in his face pierced her fragile barricades with ease and the feelings she'd been denying boiled to the surface. She knew with terrible clarity that she was falling in love with Trevor Sinclair. The shock of the realization left her speechless since her throat was clogged by something that was half sob and half hysterical laughter.

Unable to bear her silence, Trevor continued, "It's just that I don't want to let too much time pass before I see Crystal again. I don't want her to forget me or start thinking that I'm the monster who deserted her mother and refused to love her. Thanks to my father, we've missed so much. I can't tell you how hard it was to let her get on that plane this morning. If you hadn't been there beside me . . ."

His arms tightened and she buried her face against his chest, afraid of what he might read in her eyes. It was too soon for love. She was still trying to find her own identity, the person that Ken had so nearly destroyed with his rules and expectations, his way of making her feel gawky and stupid whenever she disagreed with him or tried to find something in her life that she could call her own.

"Please say yes, Diana. We can make it perfect, plan things so that we'll all have time to get to know each other as we should have years ago. If your mother won't come, we can go to Phoenix for part of the time. I know that I owe her a great debt for everything she did for Crystal, so I'd never . . ." He stopped, his fingers tightening on her upper arms as he forced her back so that she had to meet his gaze. "You have to trust me, Diana. We've come too far to go back."

Looking into his eyes, she wanted nothing more than to say yes and then to kiss him until the world vanished again but, of course, she couldn't. This wasn't the kind of decision that should be made in the heat of passion—or the aftermath, either.

Knowing she couldn't evade his question, she answered the only way she could. "I can't make any commitments until I talk to Mom and Crystal, Trevor. It's not just up to me. You have to understand . . ." Her throat closed. Suddenly all the emotions that had warred within her since she met Trevor spilled over, flooding her cheeks with tears that she hadn't even known were coming.

"Darling, oh darling, don't cry. Of course I'll wait for your decision." Trevor pulled her into his arms again and she felt the tender touch of his lips against her forehead and hair as she sobbed on his shoulder.

What the hell had he said? he asked himself as he stroked her heaving shoulders, feeling helpless and frustrated. All he'd asked for was trust. All he'd wanted was to give her a wonderful Christmas, a family Christmas in paradise.

Family? The word slowed his hands. Was that why she was so upset? Had she expected something else, something just between the two of them? He closed his eyes, not sure exactly what he wanted or how he felt. When he kissed her, she set him on fire; but now . . . He couldn't imagine being without her, but at the same time, he wasn't sure what he wanted from her. Or what he had to give her.

As her sobs eased, embarrassment spread through Diana. She never cried, at least not in public. She'd been proud of the fact that Ken had never seen her cry, had never known how deeply he hurt her with his accusations and recriminations. Trevor was going to think she was some kind of helpless basket case.

She fumbled in her pocket, seeking a tissue, then accepted Trevor's handkerchief, using it to hide her face as she moved out of his arms. "I'm sorry. I don't know what came over me. I never cry like this."

"You've never been through anything like this, Diana. Neither have I. I think we're both exhausted by Crystal's visit and . . . and by everything that's happened since. We'll talk tomorrow."

There was withdrawal in his tone; she felt it even though he hadn't moved an inch. Pain surged through her; she didn't want him to go! The urgency of her need to remain in his arms surprised her, but it was real—as real as what had happened between them on the beach. That thought sobered her and warned her not to trust her own instincts. Though she felt as if a part of her was being torn away, she moved out of his comforting arms.

"I think maybe you're right. We both need some time to get our lives back into perspective. If you don't mind, I think I'll go up to bed now." Her knees were shaking as she got to her feet, but she managed to cross the room and climb the stairs without looking back.

Once she was in the shadowy upper hall, however, she couldn't resist. Her heart contracted painfully when she realized that he was now holding his head in his hands. Was he hurting, too? But why? It frightened her to realize that she might never know what went on inside the mind and heart of the man who'd come to mean so much to her.

The phone began to ring even as she closed her bedroom door, which was just as well, she told herself. Let his other life claim him. That was where he really belonged, just as she belonged back in Pleasant Valley sending out job applications and making positive steps toward insuring her own future—a future that probably wouldn't have much to do with spending time in paradise with a pirate who made love like . . .

Cursing her own longing, she blinked back fresh tears just as she heard footsteps in the hall. Trevor's tone was worried as he tapped on her door and said, "Diana, your mother's on the telephone. I think you'd better talk to her. You can take it in the office."

A stab of fear dried her eyes and her heart was pounding as she opened the door and brushed by Trevor.

"If you need anything, I'll be downstairs . . ." His voice was gentle, filled with concern and the kindness she'd come to treasure.

She tried to speak, but her mouth was too dry, so she simply nodded and stepped into the office. Her hand was shaking as she picked up the receiver and sank down into the chair. "Mom, what's wrong?"

"What's wrong? Everything is wrong! Why are you still there? Crystal called to tell me the news about Wilding and she said you'd decided to stay on." Her mother's voice was hoarse with emotions and she began to cough immediately.

Guilt swirled around Diana as images of her passionate time on the beach at Hibiscus Cove filled her mind. Why had Mom called now when she was still so confused? She'd planned to talk to her tomorrow, to give her the good news and to do her best to convince her that it was good news.

"Diana, what's happening to you? You aren't falling under that monster's spell, are you? Remember what he did to Eileen. Don't trust him, he . . ." Another bout of coughing ended the tirade.

Knowing she had to calm her mother's wild fears, Diana forced her own feelings aside. "I stayed on because we needed to work out the details of Crystal's education. We didn't have much time while she was here. I'll be leaving probably tomorrow or the next day, depending on when I can get reservations."

Silence greeted her words, which, she suspected, was good. At least that meant her mother was listening. She tried to think of more statements that she could make, but none came to mind. She already knew that defending Trevor was a waste of time and breath; meeting him and getting to know him would be the only way to convince her mother that she'd been wrong all these years.

Unable to bear the silence any longer, Diana decided to try a subject she knew they could agree on. "Was Crystal real excited when she called you?"

"She sounded happy." There was another silence, followed by a sigh. "She said she had a super time on the island and that her . . . that Trevor Sinclair was nothing like she expected."

"I think you'll agree when you meet him." Diana couldn't help smiling with relief. Trevor would be pleased to know that Crystal had called him her father.

"I doubt that will ever happen." Her mother's icy tone killed her smile.

"He's going to be part of Crystal's life from now on, Mom. I think you should give him a chance. None of this was his fault." She stopped herself. "We'll talk about it when I get back, okay?"

Her mother's weary sigh made Diana's heart ache even though she still felt sure she'd done the right thing by uniting Trevor with his daughter. The right thing for Crystal, she amended as she said her goodbyes; for herself, she wasn't so sure. In fact, the only thing she did know for sure was that she needed to get away from Trevor before she made a serious mistake—if she hadn't already.

Once she'd hung up the receiver, she stayed where she was, forcing herself to look around the room, to study the photographs of Amanda that she preferred to ignore. As she faced Trevor's past, she remembered an incident from early in her relationship with Ken. She'd asked him about his first wife and he'd told her in loving terms just how perfectly suited they'd been. It was only now that she realized that much of what had gone wrong between them had been because she wasn't like his first wife and had no desire to change.

"Is everything all right?" Trevor's voice forced her out of the past and she got to her feet at once, surprised that she hadn't heard him approach.

"Crystal called Mom after we talked to her."

"She's upset that Crystal's going to Wilding?" Trevor's concerned frown deepened.

"She's upset that I didn't go home with Crystal."

"Oh."

"I told her I would leave as soon as I could get on a plane." She spoke quickly, ignoring the pain that came from the glint of guilt she'd seen in his eyes. In spite of her own confused feelings, she hated the thought that he felt guilty about what they'd shared—that he might be sorry. No matter how much trouble their lovemaking might create in the future, she knew she'd never be sorry it had happened.

"Must you go so soon?" Trevor leaned on the door-jamb, effectively blocking her exit from the office.

Her heart leaped at the idea that he might want her to stay, but she nodded. "I left a lot of things undone when I came."

"What about Christmas?"

"That's something I need to talk to Mom about and I think it would be better if I did it in person." Right after she got her emotions back under control, if she could.

She sensed his tension, but after a moment, Trevor nodded and moved back into the hall. Within moments, she was alone in her room again. And lonely—very specifically lonely. Memories of the magic she and Trevor had shared filled the restless hours before she fell asleep and created wonderfully tender and erotic dreams for her.

Morning dawned bright and sunny and full of promise, the kind of day that made her want to forget everything but the special world she and Trevor could share. Could she steal one more day? It seemed likely that she wouldn't be able to get on a plane before tomorrow, so . . .

She shook off the temptation, well aware that every moment she spent with Trevor would just make the leaving more difficult. And she had to leave. She had to move on and find her own life and world. Someday, when he'd left his grief behind and she was back on her feet, maybe . . .

Diana ground her teeth, trying hard to remember that daydreams seldom came true and that wishing was for those who still believed in happy endings and love triumphing over all. The fact that she'd once been that naive didn't help. She had the scars to prove just how wrong she'd been.

Since it was mid-morning by the time she made her way downstairs, Diana was surprised to find Trevor alone in the kitchen. Her heart did a flip when he looked up and gave her his devastating pirate's grin. "I was beginning to wonder if you were going to sleep till noon," he teased, pouring coffee for her.

"I had a lot of plans to make." She sipped the hot liquid without tasting it, mesmerized by his eyes. They were glinting with gold highlights this morning, a sign she'd learned meant that he was excited about something. "What's up?"

"Can I talk you into staying one more day?"

"Why?" She avoided his eyes, not wanting him to guess that he could probably talk her into almost anything this morning.

"Well, I called Denver last night and the company jet can pick us up tomorrow morning."

"The company jet?" It took her a second longer to realize what else he'd said. "Us?"

"I've decided that it's time I went back. Harlan shouldn't have to take care of all the details of the merger and I do need to make a number of legal changes to acknowledge my daughter's existence, so . . ." He let it trail off. "Does it matter to you? It just means another day on the beach and the plane can take you to whatever city you prefer; you'll just be able to skip the hassle of trying to get on a plane out of Nassau."

Diana stared out the open door toward the beach, which sparkled with promise. Another day in paradise. Or more important, another day with Trevor. There was no way she could turn it down. "I'd be happy to accept a ride to Denver. That'll work out fine; I'm sure I can catch a flight from there to Phoenix."

"Phoenix?" His gaze narrowed.

"I need to reassure Mom."

"Let me come with you. We could talk to her together. Once she hears my side of the story . . ."

Diana was already shaking her head, appalled at the idea. Facing her mother was going to be difficult enough, considering how she felt about Trevor. To have him with her would make it impossible. "It won't work, Trevor. She's not well and . . . Please just trust me, it'll work out better if I talk to her first."

His frown told her that he didn't want to accept her words, but after a moment, he sighed and nodded. "So shall I call and have the plane here tomorrow morning?"

"Yes." There was so much more she wanted to say, but at that moment, Louise came up on the back porch, her wide smile encompassing them both, ending their time alone.

Since Louise always arrived full of gossip and news, the rest of the morning passed easily, the leftover strain between Trevor and Diana fading as their earlier comfortable relationship reasserted itself. There were plans to make and packing to do and, as long as she kept her mind off those incendiary moments on the beach, she could almost pretend everything was back to normal.

Except when their eyes met or Trevor touched her. All it took was a smoldering gaze from him and her breathing stopped and her heart pounded so loudly she was sure Louise would hear it in the next room. She waited impatiently for him to say something, to give her some sign that last night's lovemaking had changed him as much as it had changed her, but there was nothing. By late afternoon, she was beginning to feel as if she'd dreamed the whole thing. What was worse, she wasn't sure whether she should be relieved or insulted.

When Louise finally left about six, Diana felt the tightening of anticipation in her stomach. Now that they were alone in the house . . . The shrilling of the phone cut through her thoughts, derailing the erotic fantasies that danced around in her mind at the prospect of finally having Trevor's undivided attention. She started to reach for the wall phone, but the ringing had already stopped, telling her that Trevor had answered the phone in his office.

Sighing, she turned her attention to the food that Louise had left in the oven. Trevor had suggested an early dinner, so she might as well set the kitchen table. Maybe while they ate, they could talk. Her throat closed, making it clear that swallowing would be tricky if that was Trevor's plan.

She was still staring at the checkered tablecloth when she heard Trevor's footsteps on the stairs. He stopped in the doorway. "If you're getting ready to set the table, move to the dining room. Harlan's on the plane and they'll be landing in about ten minutes. I have to go pick him up."

A shiver chased down her spine as she caught a glimpse of his face. He didn't look happy. "Is something wrong?"

Trevor raked a hand through his hair, tumbling the thick black waves over his forehead in a way that set her pulse to racing. "Problems with the merger. He figured we could get a head start on the plane."

He wasn't meeting her gaze, but she couldn't be sure whether it was intentional or not. It hurt to realize that she still didn't know him well enough. She forced her brain into action. "Well, you go ahead and meet him, and I'll make sure everything is ready here. And what about the pilot? Will he be joining us, too?"

"Sam's got a girl on the island, so we won't see him until takeoff time tomorrow." Trevor's easy grin didn't touch the guarded look in his eyes, but he sounded sincere as he continued, "I'm glad you'll have a chance to meet Harlan. He's like family and . . . I'd like the two of you to get to know each other since we'll probably be spending time together in the future." He hesitated a moment, then added, "Because of Crystal."

Diana nodded, fighting a sense of loss. This definitely wasn't what she wanted to hear. Last night, they'd shared much more than just their concern and love for Crystal. Was this his way of telling her just how little it had meant to him? She fought to keep the pain from showing in her face. "I'm anxious to meet him."

Trevor watched for a moment as Diana began stacking the dishes to carry them to the dining room. Her features were composed, her expression properly polite and interested, but the fire had gone out of her eyes and he wasn't sure why. Did she think Harlan's arrival was his idea? But surely after last night she must realize that . . .

That what? Hell, he didn't know how he felt about last night or about what might have happened tonight if Harlan hadn't decided to show up. He swallowed a sigh. Maybe what Harlan had to tell him would make a difference, ease the strain that seemed to be growing between him and Diana. Something sure needed to.

In spite of her doubts about the evening, Diana found herself liking Harlan Cole. Though he lacked Trevor's sexy impact, he was both attractive and charming, not to mention friendly. During dinner he'd even asked about her job search and seemed to listen sympathetically when she described her problems in the current job market.

Still, she was glad when ten o'clock came and she could excuse herself and go up to bed. She'd had more than enough of listening to them talk about the merger. Though they'd done their best to include her in the conversation, she knew that she was keeping them from working on it. Besides, she was still far too conscious of Trevor's every movement and it was getting harder and harder to cover her distraction.

Was this what she had to look forward to? she asked her reflection in the mirror as she prepared for bed. She and Trevor would have to continue to see each other because of Crystal, a prospect that had excited her earlier but now seemed more of a problem. She needed desperately to know how he felt and she hadn't a clue.

Of course, she didn't really know how she felt either, she admitted later as she watched the shadows of the night cross her ceiling. So maybe Harlan's arrival was a blessing. It was, after all, giving them both a break from the intensity of the attraction between them. Time to cool off and forget the magic; time to realize that what they'd shared had to be an illusion, a lovely dream that had no place in the real world.

She finally slipped into sleep, sure that she could protect her vulnerable heart long enough to escape her foolish attraction to Trevor. Once she was back home, taking charge of her own life, the magic would lose its potency and she'd be able to smile and simply enjoy the experience without expecting anything else. Like love.

Trevor enjoyed the flight. In spite of his doubts, he'd found taking back the reins of ATS Industries more rewarding than painful. Harlan's occasional references to Amanda brought more good memories than bad and it felt great to be busy. Being in control also made it easier to deal with his confusion over how he felt about Diana.

Not that she seemed her usual open self. He swallowed a sigh. Maybe she was just worried about seeing her mother and the fight she obviously expected. Or was she trying to figure a way around their sharing the Christmas vacation? That thought tormented him whenever he took time to think about it. She and her mother had no right to make Crystal's decisions. If his daughter wanted to be with him . . .

He controlled his frustration as they approached Denver. He even managed a smile as he settled beside Diana. They needed to talk further about the holidays and he knew just the place for the discussion. "Will you have dinner with me after we land, Diana?" he asked. "I already had Sam make a hotel reservation for you, and we'll be arriving fairly soon so . . ." He let it trail off, suddenly aware of a change in her expression. For some reason, she didn't look pleased.

"You asked someone to make a hotel reservation for me?"

"Sam didn't mind." Trevor frowned, not sure why Diana sounded angry.

"I thought you understood that I was hoping to catch an evening flight from Denver to Phoenix."

"But you must already be exhausted. I remember how jet-lagged you were when you arrived on Bellington, so I . . ." The memory brought a wave of heat as he remembered a whole lot more than how tired she'd been. He forced his mind back to the evening ahead. "Besides, we have a number of things to discuss and I thought dinner would give us time."

"That's very kind of you, but if I can get on a flight, I would really prefer . . ."

Her stubbornness was beginning to irritate him. She was acting as if she wanted to get away from him. Trevor swallowed a sigh, realizing that he'd have to give her a better reason for staying. "Please, Diana, I asked Harlan to do some checking on job prospects among our various companies and he's come up with several positions that you might want to consider. I thought we could talk about them tonight."

Trevor watched her, anticipating her excitement, enthusiasm; but she just looked at him, her blue eyes dark and stormy. She took several deep breaths, then shook her head as though trying to clear it. "Are you saying that you asked Harlan to find me a job in one of your companies?"

He'd done exactly that, but from the expression on her face, he decided that he wouldn't admit it—especially not the fact that he'd asked before Harlan had decided to fly out to confer with him. "Well, you told him yourself that you were having a hard time finding a teaching position, so I thought it might help if you had a sort of interim job. Unless, of course, you happened to like it and decide to stay on with ATS Industries.''

Again he waited in vain for her happy acceptance. In fact, he was beginning to wonder if she was ever going to speak to him again, when she gave him the most insincere smile he'd ever seen on her face and said, "Thank you very much for thinking of me, but I will find my own job and my own hotel if I can't get a flight out of Denver. You've done more than enough already."

TEN

It took all her concentration not to scream or cry as they made the final approach to Denver's Stapleton Airport. How could he have done this to her? How could he have just assumed that she'd jump at the chance to take his charity? Did he think just because she'd asked him to help Crystal, she expected him to help her whole family? That thought was bad enough, but shivers that had nothing to do with the cold air that entered the plane the moment the door was opened shook her entire body when another possibility crossed her mind.

Was Trevor just like Ken? Did he see her as another Amanda, someone he could train to share his interest in business as well as his bed? Her stomach heaved at the thought. She'd tried so hard to please Ken and ended up losing herself; no way could she do the same with Trevor. Or any other man. If he didn't want her the way she was . . .

And if he didn't want her? The pain from that thought made her hurry off the plane, unable to trust herself not to cry if he even called her name. Or to be sure that she wouldn't give in if he begged her to stay. Because, God help her, no matter how wrong he was for her, she did want to stay. A part of her still wanted to believe that everything would make sense if she could just spend one more evening with him.

She wasn't allowed to escape. Trevor caught her arm before she'd gone a half-dozen steps. "Diana, what's wrong?"

When she turned to face him, she was shocked at the pain that was visible in his face. Had she done that? But how? And why? Why should he care whether she accepted his help? Her heart leaped at the possibility that she might actually mean something to him; then she forced the hope away. She dared not trust him or herself.

She did her best to keep her tone businesslike and polite so he wouldn't guess that she was dying inside. "Nothing is wrong, Trevor, except that I'm in a hurry to get to Phoenix. You've made it very clear that you're eager to make plans for Christmas with Crystal and that can't be done until I've talked to my mother."

"Surely you're not in too much of a hurry to wait for your luggage?" His grin and teasing tone might be a facade, but the memories they evoked shattered her protective shell as easily as a bullet would shatter glass.

"Oh, I guess I didn't . . ." She couldn't finish the excuse, because she really didn't know what to say. Besides, he'd taken her arm and his touch was doing weird and wonderful things to her insides.

"Come on, I'll walk you to the ticketing area and see what flights are available. Then Sam will deliver all your belongings to the proper airline. Or do you want me to keep the boxes of gifts here in Denver until you're ready to go back to Iowa?" He spoke casually and didn't even look at her, but she sensed the tension behind his words. Could that mean he wanted to see her again?

"I'd forgotten all about the gifts." She frowned, suddenly wearied at the prospect of trying to handle the added burden of the three large boxes that Louise had supplied to hold her many treasures from the straw market. "I should have just made arrangements to have them shipped straight home from the island."

"I can still make the arrangements, if that's what you want." Trevor stopped, his hold on her arm forcing her to face him. "I just want to help you, Diana, please believe that. If you're not ready to talk, I can wait. Just please don't feel that you have to run away from me. And don't misunderstand my having hotel reservations made for you or trying to help you find a job. That's the way I treat my friends, nothing more."

His stern expression sent a chill through her, but there was no anger in his eyes. In fact, she couldn't read any emotion in his expression and that hurt. Once again, Trevor Sinclair had become a stranger to her, a stranger with whom she just might be falling in love.

Knowing that she was in the wrong and needed to say something, Diana took a deep breath and, doing her best to hide her own feelings, managed a slightly embarrassed smile. "I'm sorry if I overreacted. You've been very kind and I do appreciate your thoughtfulness, but I'm used to handling things myself and . . ." She paused to swallow the mocking laughter that rose in her throat as she remembered just how poorly she'd handled her life to this point.

Trevor waited, unwilling to ease her obvious discomfort since his own was so strong. He hated the closed look of her face, the way she seemed to have drawn back into herself. Though he wasn't sure exactly how he felt about her, he damned well wasn't going to let her go this easily. She'd changed his world the moment she'd entered it and he wanted very much to know what was coming next between them.

Diana ground her teeth, realizing that he wasn't going to accept her rather vague apology out of hand. Which wasn't all bad, she decided, since it meant that whatever happened next would be up to her. The question was, what did she want? It took her exactly three seconds to make up her mind. She might need time to think now, but she definitely wanted to see Trevor again.

"I guess I'll probably be flying home through Denver, so I could pick up my boxes on my way back. If you don't mind storing them for a few days."

"No problem at all." He started walking again, but not before she'd glimpsed the relief in his eyes. "You can let me know when you'll be in town and we can make arrangements for the transfer. Meanwhile, let's see what we can find out about flights to Phoenix."

Her flight wasn't nearly long enough for Diana to decide what to tell her mother. Fortunately, she hadn't had time to call her aunt and uncle before her flight took off, so no one knew she was coming, a fact that enabled her to spend the rest of the night worrying alone in a hotel near the airport. She still hadn't reached a decision when her Aunt Betty pulled up in front of the hotel and Mom got out of the car.

"Are you all right, Diana?" After hugging Diana, her mother held her at arm's length, her worried gaze making it clear that she was deeply concerned.

"I'm fine, Mom, really. I just caught a late flight out of Denver and didn't want to disturb everybody when I got in."

"You couldn't have called from that island?" The chill in Mom's voice made it clear that her opinion of Trevor Sinclair hadn't changed a bit.

"We flew back in a corporate jet, so I had no idea what time I'd get to Denver or even if I'd be able to get a flight out when we did land."

"We?" Her mother stiffened.

The time to take charge had come, Diana decided, as she put her luggage in the trunk, then faced her mother with a smile that felt like a mask. "It's a long story and it can wait. Right now I want to know how you're doing. You look so much better. What does the doctor say?''

Her mother wasn't distracted for long, but by the time Diana had listened to all the good news about her mother's improving health, she actually felt ready to begin. She had a lot to tell Mom and most of it was wonderful news, whether Mom believed it or not.

Trevor wandered around the apartment without really seeing it. Restlessness ate at him, keeping him from accomplishing anything. He hadn't sorted the piles of mail. He hadn't made any arrangements for the storage of the three large boxes sitting in the middle of the living room. He hadn't even read beyond the first page of the three reports Harlan had left with him.

He glared at the clock. It was nearly noon. Diana would have told her mother by now. Why hadn't she called? His stomach knotted with frustration. He should be there, explaining to the woman himself. He didn't need someone to smooth the way for him; the truth should be enough to win Mrs. Johnson over. It had worked on Diana and Crystal, hadn't it?

He reached for the telephone, ready to set up a flight to Phoenix, then pulled his hand back. What would Diana do if he just arrived? He wasn't sure, but he had a hunch she wouldn't like it. He wondered again just how deeply her "ex" had wounded her and what he could do to make her trust him.

If only she'd been willing to consider one of the jobs Harlan had suggested. If she had a job in Denver, he'd be able to see her every day, take her out to dinner, spend time getting to know her better. Was that why she'd refused? Frustration sent him on another circuit of the room. They needed to talk and they weren't going to be able to settle anything if she was in Phoenix and he was in Denver.

* * *

"I still find it hard to believe." Sarah Johnson stared out the car window. "Eileen never said anything about a modeling career or going to New York or . . ."

"Did she tell you where she stayed during the months before Crystal was born?" Diana rubbed the back of her neck, fighting the sense of futility that was beginning to get to her. She'd never known Mom to be so stubborn, so unwilling to accept reality. The back-seat seemed to crowd them together.

"Not much. She said she spent some time in California and, of course, Crystal was born out there; but . . ."

"Do you know where she used to go when she left on her vacations from Pleasant Valley?" Diana pressed on.

Her mother glared at her, then shook her head, suddenly looking her age. "She never wanted to talk about it. And I, well, I was afraid to press her for answers. I thought she might just leave and never come back. She wasn't like you; there was always a restlessness inside her. I thought he'd caused it by deserting her that way, but I suppose she was always different."

"A free spirit?" Diana had her own memories, but she couldn't help being stung by her mother's words. Once she'd prided herself on being the dependable daughter, but now that she'd discovered the magic of taking risks . . .

"Maybe. Or maybe she just didn't know what she wanted out of life. She was never very happy, that I do know. That's why I've been so worried about Crystal. What if having him for a father makes her unhappy? What if she goes off with him and never comes back to us?"

"Trevor's not like that. He would never let Crystal hurt us." The words were out before she could stop them and she knew at once that defending him so vehemently had been a mistake.

Suspicion flared in her mother's eyes. "He's won you over, too, hasn't he? That's why you're so sure that he's good for Crystal. You've fallen under his spell just the way Eileen did.''

"Don't be silly, Mom, I just got to know him and . . ." She let it trail off, unable to lie.

Her mother turned away, her expression heavy with disgust. "I can't believe it. First you destroy a marriage that's perfect for you, claiming that you have to find yourself—whatever that means. Then what you find is the man who ruined your sister's life."

Diana opened her mouth, angry protests flooding her mind; after a moment, however, she closed it without speaking. Mom hadn't been able to understand why Ken Foster's controlling ways had nearly destroyed her before, so there was no reason to expect that she would now. Besides, it didn't take a psychologist to realize that Mom was more scared than angry at her.

She assumed her most positive expression, hoping that her mother wouldn't detect the doubts behind it. "Once you've met Trevor, you'll change your mind about him. He's really an extremely nice man."

"What makes you think I have any intention of meeting him?" Her mother's words were belligerent, but Diana could detect the curiosity in her eyes.

"I suppose that's up to you; but he is going to be a part of Crystal's life from now on, so you'll miss out on a lot if you don't give him a chance."

"Thanks to you." Sarah's anger had rekindled.

Diana nodded. "Thanks to me, Crystal will be going to Wilding in the fall. Thanks to me, she no longer feels rejected by a man who never saw her. She has a father to turn to, someone who will protect her and care for her no matter what. I think that's important. I loved my daddy a lot and I'm glad she won't be cheated out of the feeling completely."

"What if he hurts her?"

"What if he doesn't? What if he gives her all the love she's craved through the years? What if he makes her life better than it's been for a while?" Diana pushed on, even though she knew she was getting into dangerous territory. She'd run away from facing the results of her own actions long enough.

"You mean since your divorce." This time her mother's tone was gentle.

Diana sighed and pushed back her hair. "I didn't realize how Crystal felt about Ken until we were on the island. I was hurting so bad, I never realized my divorce upset her so much."

"Crystal thought she finally had the family she'd always wanted." Her mother confirmed her worst fears.

"She told you that?"

Sarah shook her head. "I doubt she was completely aware of it herself. I just saw how close they were when I was there for Christmas and, of course, she was as stunned as I was when you made your little announcement in the spring."

"Well, I think she's pretty much over that now. I imagine Ken dropped his fatherly act as soon as I left, so I doubt she has any illusions now about how he really felt toward her." Bitterness welled up inside her as she realized how hurt Crystal must have been when she returned to school in the fall to find her status completely changed.

"What do you mean his act? The man adored you both, it was obvious every moment I was there. All he wanted . . ."

Though she wasn't sure it would do any good, Diana stopped her mother with a gesture. "It was obvious every moment he had an audience. The rest of the time he spent instructing me or correcting my errors. Unless, of course, he was giving me the rules for my next performance." She took a deep breath, then tried to imitate Ken's very proper diction and tone. "The world expects no less than perfection of Mrs. Ken Foster. You must always be a credit to me and my position, my dear. Anything less would be unacceptable."

Her mother's expression changed slowly to reflect the horror dawning in her eyes. "He said that to you?"

It hurt her pride to admit it, but it was too late to hide from the truth now. Her decision not to discuss the reasons for her divorce with anyone had hurt too many people. "On more than one occasion."

"I had no idea."

"No one did. Not even me at first. I thought all marriages were like that—one person guiding the other. But after a while, I couldn't take it anymore. I didn't want to be a carbon copy of his first wife. I wanted a life of my own and . . ." She let it trail off, relieved to realize that she really didn't need to say any more. Her small confession had already freed her of the last of her anger. What Ken had done or wanted simply no longer mattered?

"Why didn't you come to me?"

For a moment, she considered reminding her mother that she had tried to talk to her, then decided that it wouldn't be worth the hurt it would cause. Ken had brought enough trouble in her life, she wasn't going to give him another thought. "I figured I'd made my own mess, I should be the one to clean it up."

"Well, for what it's worth, if he treated you that way, you made the right decision." Her mother's hand was warm as it patted her arm.

Diana smiled at her as she readied herself to return to the real purpose of this discussion. "Which brings us back to Trevor and the future."

Her mother withdrew her hand. "What part of the future?"

"Christmas vacation."

"He wants to take her away from us, doesn't he? What's he going to do, show her off to all his rich friends and family?" There was no anger in her mother's voice, only a fear and pain that Diana recognized.

"He wants to spend the time with her, that's true. But you have to understand, he feels that he was cheated of all the holidays in her life until now, which is understandable. What he wants is to have her spend at least a part of her vacation on Bellington Cay again—with us, too, if you're interested.''

''What?''

''It's a beautiful place, Mom, and he has plenty of room in the house for the three of us to stay.'' Memories of the island filled her mind and with them came a longing so intense she had to clench her lips to keep from crying out. More than anything in the world, she wanted to be on the beach at Hibiscus Cove—in Trevor's arms.

Just thinking about Trevor and reliving all the wonderful moments they'd shared helped her get through the rest of the drive as her mother demanded more and more answers about him and about what had happened during the days she'd spent on the island. It was hard to hide her feelings, but she dared not let them show now, not when she was so confused herself.

Still, it was a relief when they finally reached the small house that Betty and Fred had bought three years ago, the house where Mom had been staying since early October. Diana welcomed the distraction of Fred's greeting, then excused herself to get settled in the room she and Mom would share. She wanted to give Mom time to think about all she'd told her, to get used to the idea that Trevor was going to be a part of all their lives from now on.

Diana smiled to herself. Now there was an idea that gave her chills, just as it probably did Mom, though for very different reasons. It was also a fact that she was going to have to deal with herself—once she got over the lunacy of what they'd shared on the beach. If she could get over it.

He'd waited long enough. Trevor set aside the merger papers that he'd just spent three miserable days working through and reached for the telephone. If Diana wasn't going to phone him, he was going to have to call her. There were plans to be made and Crystal was getting impatient.

He left the receiver where it was, smiling as he recalled their conversation last night. Crystal had called to tell him that the man from Wilding had contacted her; but then they'd talked for nearly an hour, covering all sorts of subjects, most of them fascinating, except for the last. That was when she'd told him that her roommate had invited her to spend part of her Christmas vacation with her family.

He raked his fingers through his hair, which he'd finally had trimmed. Crystal hadn't sounded too excited by the invitation, but he didn't want to take a chance on having her accept it. He'd suggested that she call Diana, but . . .

A sigh shook him as he realized that he didn't want Crystal to call Diana. He wanted to talk to Diana himself. He needed to talk to her. Not talking to her was driving him crazy. He kept wondering what she was doing. What she was thinking about. What her mother had said. How she felt about what had happened on the beach. What she felt. Muttering a curse, he reached for the receiver and punched in the numbers that he already knew by heart.

When she finally came on the phone, he found himself having to swallow twice before he could even speak to her. "So how is the visit going?" he asked as soon as the greetings were out of the way. "Is your mother ready to meet me yet?"

Diana caught her breath as shivers of delight spread through her at the sound of his voice. She'd gone to the phone to call him a dozen times the past few days, but each time she'd stopped herself, not sure what she'd say to him. Now she had to answer. "As ready as she'll ever be, I guess." She sounded breathless and excited, which pretty much summed up how she felt.

"How would it be if I flew in tomorrow morning? I

could take the two of you out for a long lunch and we could get acquainted."

Tomorrow. The word brought a flood of longing. "Are you sure you're not too busy with that merger?"

"I'll never be too busy for family matters." His tone was harsh, almost angry. "We have to start making plans for Christmas. Crystal's already considering spending part of the vacation with her roommate."

"You've talked to her?" Her glow chilled slightly.

"Several times, but she just told me last night about the invitation."

Diana swallowed hard. She'd talked to Crystal once, but that had been the night after she arrived and there'd been no mention of the holidays. "I guess we'd better settle things," she admitted.

"Is tomorrow all right then?"

"It'll be fine. If you can tell me when, I can borrow my aunt's car and meet you at the airport and . . ."

"I'll rent a car. Just give me directions to where you're staying and we'll take it from there." He kept his tone businesslike, though his body had tightened as soon as he heard her voice. Though he hadn't wanted to admit it even to himself, he'd missed her terribly.

With the date settled, he relaxed a little, telling her what Crystal had told him about the Wilding representative, then describing his progress on the merger. It was easy to talk to her, maybe too easy. He didn't want the conversation to end. Only the promise of seeing her tomorrow made it possible to say goodbye and break the connection.

Diana replaced the receiver slowly, not looking forward to the explanation she was going to have to give the three people waiting in the other room. It was the call she'd been expecting, but now that the moment was here, she wondered if anything would ever really work out for her.

Her mother wasn't thrilled. Diana gritted her teeth and ignored the list of reasons her mother had for not going out to lunch with Trevor. She knew she had the one reason that her mother couldn't ignore—the possibility that Crystal would go home for Christmas with Jennifer. She offered it quietly and was relieved when it ended the discussion.

Diana stood at the door watching the rental car as it pulled away. She leaned against the doorjamb, exhaustion weakening her knees and making her head pound. Or was it disappointment?

She and Trevor hadn't had a single minute alone, not from the time he arrived to pick them up until now when he'd said his farewells and shaken her hand. Her whole body throbbed with frustration at the memory. She'd wanted so much more. And so had he. She'd seen the longing in his eyes, felt it in his touch.

A wry smile touched her lips. What had they done to themselves by planning a ten-day vacation on Bellington Cay? How in the name of heaven would they survive being in the same house and not touching, not kissing, not surrendering to . . . She cursed under her breath and closed her eyes. She'd never be able to live through it.

"Well, what do you think?" Her mother's voice broke into her disturbing thoughts. "Will Crystal be happy with the arrangements?"

"She'll probably be ecstatic." Diana turned slowly, hoping the emotional turmoil wasn't visible in her face. "She adored the island and getting to know her father." She focused on her mother. "What do you think of him now?"

"He seems to really care about her. And I guess we have to accept his word about what happened between him and Eileen. I just hope . . ." She let it trail off, then shrugged. "I guess it's just all going too fast for me."

Diana nodded. She remembered the feeling only too well. So well, in fact, she decided it might be better

to change the subject before she gave herself away.
"You've got a couple of weeks to get used to the idea.
Meanwhile, I guess we'd better start thinking about the
shop. Have you heard any more from the Dahlmer
sisters?"

The change of subject helped, giving her time to
regain perspective on her wayward emotions. Talking
of home always had that effect, maybe because she'd
always felt in control of herself while she was there.
In fact, by the time she finished catching up on the
details of the sale, she ached to be back in Pleasant
Valley. Stating her need to discuss the sale with the
family lawyer, she made reservations to fly home on
Monday.

She didn't think of the boxes of gifts waiting for her
in Denver until she arrived at the Phoenix airport Monday morning—a convenient lapse of memory, one that
proved just how confused her feelings about Trevor really were. Aware that she was behaving like a coward,
she sent her family on their way, then used the pay
phone to call Trevor at the number he'd given her,
hoping that it would be his office, so she could leave
a message with his secretary.

Naturally, he answered the phone and sounded de-
lighted to hear from her—at least until she explained
why she'd called. "You what? Just an hour between
flights? Can't you get a later flight out of here?"

Her explanations about having to take the flight that
landed near Pleasant Valley were true, but somehow
they sounded lame. Maybe it was because she really
wished she could take a later flight or stay over or let
him send her the rest of the way on his corporate jet,
none of which would be a good idea since she still
wasn't sure how to handle the attraction that blazed
through her the moment she heard his voice.

"All right, I'll have someone take the boxes to the
airport and make sure they'll be on your flight out. Is

that what you want?'' He was angry. She could tell by his tone and the precise way he was speaking.

"I just didn't want to cause you any trouble, but . . .''

"Spending some time with you would be a pleasure, Diana. I thought you knew that.''

"But I have business appointments at home and I have to get back to job hunting and . . .'' She stopped herself, fighting tears. For some stupid reason, she had the feeling that she'd hurt him and the very thought made her ache inside.

"As a matter of fact, this call is rather short notice. I might not be able to get the boxes to the airport in time, so why don't I just bring them to Pleasant Valley myself, say later in the week? Maybe Friday. You'll probably have everything caught up by then, won't you?'' The challenge in his tone sent a ripple of anticipation through her and made her breath catch in her throat.

"Well, . . . ah . . . I guess I will, but . . .'' A thousand reasons why he shouldn't come flooded into her mind, but she couldn't bring herself to state them. Instead, her pulse rate leaped at the idea of seeing him again so soon.

"I'd love to see where Crystal grew up, and your mother mentioned that you have some photo albums and . . .'' The longing in his voice was irresistible, especially when she had no desire to resist.

She swallowed her doubts and questions. "That would be fine. Having you in Pleasant Valley will give me a chance to repay a little of the hospitality you extended to me on the island.''

"I'll see you Friday then. Have a good flight home.'' He kept his goodbyes short, which was just as well, as she could hear her flight being called.

It was only after she was settled on board the airplane that the full import of her actions struck her. Trevor Sinclair in Pleasant Valley? The very image was disturbing. And what was she going to do with him? She couldn't have him stay at the house, not with Mom gone. The scandal would be all over town in a few hours. It took all her self-control not to unbuckle her seat belt and get off the plane.

Once her heart stopped pounding like a demented drummer, however, she realized that it might be for the best. Once he saw how they lived, the kind of world she'd come from, he'd understand Crystal better . . . and maybe her, too. And she might see him differently there, away from his island paradise and the trappings of power that he used so casually.

The mocking laughter echoed in her head. If she believed that, why was she already counting the days until Friday and wondering if Trevor would greet her with a kiss when she picked him up at the small Pleasant Valley Airport?

ELEVEN

Though Diana had expected the time to drag, the week flew by as she worked out the details for the sale of the dress shop and did her best to put the house in order. Everything went surprisingly well, except her search for a teaching position.

The applications she'd mailed out before she went to Bellington Cay had produced nothing but refusals. No one seemed interested in hiring an English teacher with library experience or a school librarian with teaching experience. In fact, no one seemed interested in hiring her period.

Had Ken carried out his threat? She'd tried hard not to believe that he would, but now she had to wonder. He was, after all, a man with good connections in the academic world and she had worked nowhere but at Cliffton. Her stomach knotted at the thought of never being able to find a decent teaching job again.

But it couldn't be that, she told herself sternly. It was just the economy, the fact that every school was having budget trouble. After all, his power didn't reach to Pleasant Valley, and there'd been no openings here, either. Still, it was a joy to put her worries aside on Friday morning as she zipped up her parka and headed through the snowy streets to the airport to meet Trevor.

She looked wonderful. Even through the window in the dismal little building that served as an airport, her smile made his heartbeat quicken like a teenager's on his first date. It took all his self-control to keep from racing inside and grabbing her. He wanted to kiss her until . . . But, he reminded himself, he wasn't going to take any more chances with her. This time, he was going to play it slow and easy.

He shivered as he crossed the windswept area between the plane and the building, fighting to hold onto the boxes and his suitcase. His months on the island had made him much more conscious of the cold—or maybe he was just reacting to his own tension where Diana was concerned. Their time together in Phoenix had left him frustrated, miserable, and prey to doubts; he definitely didn't want this visit to have the same effect.

As she opened the door for him, Diana tried not to notice how her hands were shaking. Just seeing him again had awakened all the longing and hunger that she'd tried to subdue. He set the boxes and his suitcase down as soon as he stepped through the door, reaching out to take her hands. When his fingers closed over hers, the electricity crackled along her nerves and made her weak with longing.

"Sorry I couldn't have arranged a nicer day for you," she murmured, aware the words were meaningless but unable to speak any of the thoughts that filled her mind.

"I've been freezing ever since we left the island. Except for the day I was in Phoenix. Harlan tells me I've gotten soft." He could feel the heat that radiated from her fingers and his body tensed with longing. Her lips were a soft invitation as she looked up at him with a smile of welcome that made him feel ten feet tall.

"Did you have a good flight? I mean, no problems from the weather?" She forced her gaze away from him, afraid that he'd be able to read her feelings in her eyes, then gasped, ''Your plane is leaving!''

''Sam's heading for Chicago to drop Harlan off. He's going to be spending the weekend with a couple of possible investors in one of our newer companies.''

''Oh.'' She swallowed hard, caught between her joy at having him all to herself and dread at the thought that she would have to tell him that he couldn't possibly stay at her house.

Trevor studied her expression, sensing immediately that she was uncomfortable, though he wasn't sure why. Had she expected him to keep the plane here, ready to leave at a moment's notice? Or was she expecting to have Sam as a distraction? It was time to make his position here clear to her. ''Do I need to rent a car?''

''A car, no, of course not. You can use mine and I'll drive Mom's if we need two.'' She took a deep breath, trying to find a tactful way to state the realities of small-town life.

''Good, then we can just go drop my suitcase off at the Pleasant Valley Inn. I had my secretary make reservations for me there. I hope it's not too far from your house.'' When he saw the relief dawning in her eyes, he knew that he'd made the right decision. Much as he wanted to be near her, he had to give her the space she seemed to need right now.

''The inn's great.'' She grinned at him. ''I'd love to offer you the guest room at the house, but in this town . . . Well, it would be a major scandal.''

''I'd never want to compromise your good name that way, Diana. It's different on the island, I know. But this is your home and Crystal's. If I'm going to be part of her life and yours, we have to make it right from the beginning.''

The warmth and tenderness in his eyes made her want to slip into his arms. More than anything, she wanted to cling to him as she had on the island, to feel his lips on hers and to answer his kiss with all the passion that . . . She forced the intriguing images from her mind, barely keeping back a groan. It was going to be a long weekend, even if he did plan to sleep at the inn.

Once they were in the car, Trevor leaned back, facing her as he broached the subject that had been on his mind ever since he'd maneuvered her into inviting him to Pleasant Valley. "Have you decided what you're going to tell people about me?"

Diana met his gaze proudly. "That's not going to be a problem, since I've already told several people about you. I mean, everyone knew that Eileen wasn't married, so I thought it was only fair that they know the true story."

"How does your mother feel about that?" His pleasure shone from his eyes, warming her more than the car heater ever could.

"Uncomfortable, but she accepts the fact that it has to be this way."

"And you?"

"I just want everyone to know that Crystal has a terrific father after all." Her voice shook a little as she said the words and she had to blink back the sudden burn of tears. What was there about Trevor that touched her so deeply, more deeply than any man she'd ever known?

"I'm very glad you feel that way, Diana." His voice was soft, a caress that made her want to reach out to him once more. Since the road conditions made any such action impossible, after a moment, she cleared her throat and blinked away the emotional dampness in her eyes. This was no time to be getting all sentimental; she couldn't afford to make herself vulnerable to him again.

"So are you ready for an exciting tour of the thriving metropolis of Pleasant Valley, Iowa?"

"I'm looking forward to it. From the air, it looked

like a Christmas card town. The kind of place that's nice for a child growing up, if you know what I mean." His easy tone made it clear that he was willing to accept her effort to defuse the heat between them.

"It has its good points and it does feel like home." Torn between relief and a twinge of disappointment, Diana began describing Crystal's life here, hoping as she spoke that she'd soon be able to relax and enjoy Trevor's company as she had while they were on the island.

Much to her surprise, the special feeling of friendship did return and, because of it, their time together seemed to fly by. Though she'd expected Trevor to be bored, he appeared completely content to share her quiet life. He spent endless hours looking through the various photo albums Mom had kept through the years and seemed fascinated by the boxes of souvenirs from Crystal's childhood that she carried down from the attic.

Their only ventures out consisted of dinner at the inn Saturday night and church on Sunday morning. Both times, they were surrounded by the friendly, but curious townspeople. As expected, Trevor had no difficulty charming them and he seemed to enjoy the stories they told him—stories that sometimes embarrassed Diana, since she quite frequently figured in them.

"I had no idea you were such a daredevil," Trevor teased as Diana drove home after church. "Skinny-dipping, Diana? And with several boys. I'm impressed."

"Considering I was four at the time and remember very little beyond the fact that I couldn't sit comfortably for several days after my father heard about it, I doubt it constitutes much of an adventure. It was just a hot day and I knew I'd be in trouble if I got my clothes wet." So why was she blushing? Perhaps because that had been the first and last time she'd defied convention—at least until her visit to Bellington Cay.

"I'll bet you were adorable."

"You have me mixed up with Eileen. She was the beauty in the family; at least, until Crystal came along. I was the tomboy."

"I find that hard to believe."

Diana tightened her grip on the steering wheel as she felt his fingers touching her unruly hair, then brushing her cheek. Her throat went dry and she had a little trouble catching her breath. He'd kissed her lightly when she left him at the inn last night, but they'd both been conscious of Mr. Henley behind the desk inside, so they'd kept the caress as casual as was possible with all the electricity crackling between them.

Conscious of the growing tension, she forced a small chuckle. "Maybe you haven't been looking at the right photo albums. I'm the one with the skinned knees and pigtails."

"And the most beautiful blue eyes and sweetest smile." His voice sounded a little rough as his fingers moved under her hair to caress the nape of her neck, sending shivers through her.

Did he know how his touch affected her? Did he feel the same wild flashes of heat that moved through her like lightning, igniting all the fires she'd tried so hard to bank? Was that what he wanted? Had he come here hoping to renew the physical relationship they'd begun in Hibiscus Cove? Though she'd told herself such a thing could never be, the very idea turned her hands to ice and her heart to flame.

"I thought we'd have dinner here today," she began, fighting her weakening resolve. "I put the roast in before I left, so all I have to do is add the vegetables."

"Sounds perfect."

A whole day alone in the house with Trevor sounded dangerous and exciting, she decided, as her pulse rate leaped into high. There was an intimacy here that she hadn't felt on the island, perhaps because the lightly falling snow and freezing wind seemed to isolate them from the rest of the world. Or was the intimacy inside her, coming from the secret place in her heart that he'd touched so easily that night on the beach? The place she hadn't known existed before that magical night.

She turned into the driveway and reached for the garage door opener with a hand that shook. Never had she wanted a man so completely, so passionately. Yet how could she yield to her desire again, knowing as she did that her growing love was doomed? And how could she deny it?

Trevor started to reach out to Diana, wanting to pull her into his arms and kiss her trembling lips, but the look in her eyes stopped him. Her desire was obvious, but he could read fear and sorrow mingled with it in her expressive face. Slowly, painfully, he forced his hunger back under his control.

Am I being a fool? he asked himself as he followed her inside, sniffing the sweet scents of roasting beef as they entered the kitchen. He knew she wanted him, so why not press his advantage? A few kisses would banish her doubts and once she gave in to her passion again . . .

Then what? he asked himself bluntly. He was no boy heedlessly taking what was offered. Having known sorrow and regret, he had no desire to inflict it on others. Diana's behavior had made it clear that their lovemaking on the island had disturbed her, so whatever the cause, he had no right to make her suffer—which was why he'd vowed to win her over by waiting until she came willingly to his bed. He just hoped he didn't die of the strain before she did.

To distract himself, he focused on something Diana had mentioned at dinner last night. "Did you want me to look over the sales contract your lawyer brought over yesterday?" he asked.

Diana took his coat and hung it in the closet beside hers, glad of the excuse to keep her face turned away. His abrupt change of subject shocked her. What was going on here? What had happened to the blazing heat she'd felt flowing between them while they were in the car? Was he playing some sort of game with her emotions? Her stomach knotted at the idea.

It took her a moment to bring her mind back to his question. "I wouldn't ask except that I'm not sure about a couple of the clauses. I haven't seen a sales contract before and since the lawyer, Mr. Douglas, is representing the Dahlmer sisters, too, I thought . . ." She let it trail off, her thoughts derailed by the shock in his face.

"You're both using the same lawyer?" Trevor's frown did nothing to detract from his appeal. Even with his hair shorter and his beard trimmed, he had the sensual power of the untamed buccaneer she'd met her first night on Bellington Cay.

"He's the only one in Pleasant Valley."

"Then you'd better let me look it over. I'm no lawyer, but I've learned to spot problems—mostly because I didn't find them the first time. Starting your own business can be very educational, believe me." He looked around. "Can I help you with the dinner preparations or would you rather I look at the agreement now?"

What she really wanted was to be in his arms, but since he was offering her a perfect opportunity to get her emotions back under control, she decided to accept it. "If you don't mind, I'd really like your opinion of the contract. I'm supposed to see Mr. Douglas tomorrow morning for the signing."

Swallowing a groan of frustration, Trevor accepted the legal document and seated himself obediently in the comfortable living room. It took him nearly fifteen minutes of staring at the neatly typed lines before he finally stopped seeing Diana's face and actually began to recognize words. Shaking his head, he settled down to read.

Habit took over. Business had been his refuge for years, starting with the day after Amanda's illness had been diagnosed and continuing until the dark days following her death, when he'd finally stopped caring. By the time he became aware of Diana in the doorway between the living room and dining room, he'd made several notes and was feeling much more in control of his desire.

"Is it bad?" Diana hadn't missed the frown he'd been directing at the open document.

Trevor got to his feet, his frown vanishing. "No, there's very little wrong with the contract. I have a few suggestions that you might make to your lawyer, changes that would offer assurances to both you and the buyers; but they can wait." He set the contract on the table. "How is dinner coming? It smells terrific."

"It'll be done in about an hour. Would you like a glass of wine while we wait?" She gestured toward the decanter and glasses she'd set out this morning.

"Why don't you let me get it?" he suggested. "You've been working for hours. It's time you sat down for a while."

Diana sank down on the couch, not because she was tired, but because just looking at him here in her living room made her knees weak. He seemed so at home, as comfortable in her mother's house as he had been in his own home on the island or on the jet during their flight back. Obviously he was a man used to dominating his surroundings—and the people around him? She had a disturbing suspicion that Trevor would have no qualms about planning her life for her, if she was willing to let him. Which she most definitely was not!

Trevor brought her wine, settling on the couch beside her, his grin sending quivers of warmth through her. "I didn't get a chance to ask you yesterday, but how is your job search going? Any good prospects?"

The illusion of heat faded fast as she stared into the ruby heart of her wine glass, avoiding Trevor's too-perceptive gaze. "Not so far. It seems to be a tough market." Especially without letters of recommendation, though she didn't add that, not wanting to bring the ugliness of her divorce into their conversation.

"Well, maybe after the new year." *Back off,* he told himself, sensing her tension. Damn, but he wished she'd let him help; but her reaction before made him afraid to make an offer. To distract her, he decided to tackle another subject that was close to his heart. "Meanwhile, why don't we start making our plans for Christmas? And how about calling Crystal later? If we could come up with the dates, we could get everything settled and I can make arrangements with Sam to fly you, Crystal, and your mother to the island in the jet."

"You'd fly us out?" She caught her breath, well aware that this would solve her immediate problems of getting airline reservations during the holidays and of finding the money to pay for them.

"Of course. Your mother shouldn't have to put up with the inconvenience of changing planes or worrying about catching the interisland flight. Besides, I want all of you to arrive at the same time. That way I can have everything ready." His boyish grin did it to her again, bringing the tightness to her throat and making her eyes sting with unshed tears. He looked so genuinely excited by the prospect, he was irresistible.

Her doubts faded as she leaned forward, ready to hear all about the plans he had in mind. For now, she wanted to believe in the magical season ahead and to share all the joy it promised.

Dinner passed in a haze of laughter as Trevor suggested more and more exotic diversions that they could include in the ten days they were to be on Bellington Cay. His increasingly wild scenarios showed her a whimsical side of him she never would have suspected, melting away her reserves and making her forget her doubts and fears.

Her sides ached from laughing as she finally got to her feet and began to clear the table. "I just don't see my mother taking up scuba diving, but I think Crystal would love it.''

"Your mother might have an adventurous side you don't suspect,'' he teased, rising to help her as though it were the most natural thing in the world. ''But if not, I'll bet she'd enjoy a shopping safari and the dinner cruise will be fun for everyone.''

''We're all going to need a vacation to recover from this visit,'' she predicted as she put the food away, then turned to find him standing so close behind her that she would have stumbled had he not caught her in a gentle embrace.

''Is it too much?'' The intensity of his gaze put her heart into overdrive and held her breathless.

Since she knew he meant the question to cover far more than just the plans they'd made, she answered from the heart. ''It sounds like a dream vacation in paradise.''

''That's what I want it to be, Diana, for you as well as for your mother and Crystal. I want to make up for all the lonely holidays we've had and build something special for the future. I want it to be right.''

For a moment she felt a little flicker of fear, remembering that Ken had said something similar when he suggested inviting her mother and Crystal to spend last Christmas with them. But she knew this wasn't the same. Ken had wanted the appearance of family because he felt it was expected; Trevor was seeking the genuine emotions. He wanted to make the people he cared about happy. And he'd come up with an incredible number of wonderful ways to do it.

''Do you think it will work out?'' He lifted one hand to brush back the wayward tendrils of hair that fell over her cheeks, then caressed the skin they'd covered. The kitchen suddenly seemed very quiet, making her conscious of the ragged sound of her own breathing and the pounding of her heart.

His lips were so close, his hazel eyes blazing golden

with desire as he bent his head a little more. A quiver of warning told her she must pull away now, but she couldn't move. Slowly, deliberately, she licked her lips. Her eyes were already growing heavy, weighted with desire. "How could it be anything but perfect, when you've planned it with so much love?"

Since her hands had somehow found their way around him, she felt the shiver that shook his strong body just before his lips claimed hers in a kiss that made the world disappear. She opened her heart to him as he deepened the caress, answering her eager hunger with his own as he pressed her body ever closer, letting her feel the strength of his desire, his need.

"I want you, Diana." His breath whispered against her ear, sending chills of longing through her. "I've wanted you every moment since that night in the Cove. You're so sweet, so beautiful, and so sexy."

She leaned back just enough so she could meet his gaze, reading the honest emotions in his eyes, the same emotions that surged through her like a volcanic eruption. He was telling her that it was up to her, she realized, giving her the choice of ending it now before they made love again. Yet there was no choice for her, not really, for it was already far too late to deny her feelings.

With her throat too dry for words, she simply took his hand and led him through the house and up the stairs to her room, the room she'd never shared with any man before. Once there, she met his gaze as she slowly began to remove her clothes, her head high even as her hands shook and her fingers proved clumsy.

"Now you," she whispered when she stood naked before him.

Though she wasn't touching him, she could see the emotional shiver that moved over him as he quickly stripped off his clothing, baring his magnificent body to her greedy gaze. A matching quiver shook her as she stepped into his arms and offered her eager mouth to him. Once their lips were sealed in mutual need, he lifted her and, never breaking the kiss, carried her to the bed.

Once they were nestled in the soft quilt, their love-making was less frenzied than it had been on the beach. Now they took the time to explore each other with care and tenderness, joyously fanning the flames of their desire until it exploded in their final union, consuming them, fusing their bodies and their hearts into one.

It seemed an eternity later that Diana opened her eyes. Though the cold wind rattled the windows of her room, she felt warm and safe cradled in Trevor's arms, the quilt now wrapped around them like a cocoon. She rubbed her cheek against the soft curls on his chest, breathing in the musky scent of him, feeling a part of him in a way she never had before.

"I thought you might be sleeping." His fingers moved lazily over her, coming to rest on her breast.

"I was drifting in the clouds. I never knew it could be like that. I wasn't sure I'd ever come back to earth."

"I'm not sure I want to. Being out there with you is so very special. You've made me feel alive again, Diana, made me want to live and feel and . . . It's wonderful."

"Perfect," she agreed, nuzzling through the curls to taste the nipple hidden there, intrigued to feel it react to her touch and at the same time feel her own desire reviving. "I think we should . . ."

The shrilling of the telephone cut through her dreamy words, scattering her thoughts. She started to pull away, swallowing a sigh of frustration. "Don't go." Trevor's arms tightened around her. "Let them call back."

She ached to do as he asked, but the habits of a lifetime were too strong. "It could be Mom or Crystal."

He sighed, but his arms loosened at once, freeing her. Feeling naked as she hadn't earlier, she grabbed her robe off the closet door before she headed across the hall to answer the phone, which was in her mother's room.

She was shivering by the time she returned to tell him that the call was for him. "Take the quilt," she advised, draping it over his shoulders when he stood up. "You'll need it, it's cold in there."

It was cold in here, too, she realized, as she watched him disappear through the door across the hall. She hugged herself, feeling a draft that came from within rather than from the window or the door that stood open to the hall. Suddenly she felt very much alone in the dimming of the late winter afternoon and unshed tears burned behind her eyelids as she tried to blink them away.

Why was she feeling so abandoned? She could still hear the rumble of Trevor's voice across the hall, although she couldn't make out the words. Then she realized the truth. Harlan had called him here and that was enough to tell her that his real life was summoning him back—a life in which she neither had nor wanted any part.

Swallowing a sob, she picked up her discarded clothes and pulled them on, then sank down at her dressing table to try to tame the chaos of her hair. It was hard to do while she was trying to avoid meeting her own gaze in the mirror, but she managed to subdue it before a sound drew her eyes to the doorway.

"You're dressed." The disappointment in Trevor's face would have amused her had she been less anxious about losing what they'd just shared.

"I was cold." The words were true, but when their eyes met, she knew that he saw beyond them to her doubts and fears.

"I'm sorry he interrupted us."

"Is it a crisis?" She couldn't bear the sadness in his face, yet her own need to protect herself kept her from rushing into his arms again. She'd given him her heart;

she couldn't give him any more without losing herself completely.

"I'm afraid so. That's why he called today. He and Sam will be picking me up first thing in the morning. If I don't do some fancy maneuvering right away, we could lose the merger and ATS Industries would take a heavy hit. I can't let that happen."

Her chill deepened as she watched him dress. The devil-may-care pirate-lover had vanished, replaced by a solemn, slightly weary stranger who didn't need her tenderness or caring. Unable to bear the sight, she looked down at her hairbrush, prying her fingers loose from the handle so she could set it back on the dresser.

"I'm sorry, Diana. I'd hoped that we'd have another day or so. I thought I might be able to accompany you to your meeting with the lawyer and whatever else you have to take care of here. I really wanted to spend more time here."

The genuine sadness in his voice broke through the invisible barricade that she'd sensed between them. The remote stranger disappeared as she met Trevor's gaze and lost herself in the memories of all they'd just shared. "I'm sorry, too."

She wanted to say more, but her throat was too tight for the words to get through. It was easier to speak with her lips as Trevor took her in his arms. She clung to him, seeking in his kiss the special oneness that they'd forged in the fire of their passion, now needing it to feel complete. She was dizzy with longing by the time he lifted his lips from hers.

"Why don't you come with me, Diana? You could call the lawyer from Denver, work out the details of the sale on the phone. I don't want us to be apart." His arms tightened, crushing her against him. "I need you in my life."

She buried her face against his chest, feeling the violent pounding of his heart as it echoed her own. A part of her ached to accept his invitation, to surrender to her desperate need for him; but a saner voice in her mind shouted a warning at the mere thought. He wanted her, maybe even needed her, but that could never be enough. Without his love, being with him would only be a sweet, doomed torment.

"Diana, please say yes. We can have a great time in Denver. And you don't have that much to take care of here, do you?" He stepped back, letting her go so that he could cup her face, lifting her head so that she had to meet his gaze.

"I can't, Trevor. I have so many details to take care of for Mom. And for myself. Besides, you'll be busy with the merger. I'd just be in the way . . ." The excuses weighed heavy on her lips, but she couldn't tell him the truth. She couldn't admit her own vulnerability, not until she was sure she could trust him not to break her heart.

"Maybe you could help out. If you'd give it a try, you might discover that you enjoy the business world. It can be very exciting and rewarding. When we were starting ATS Industries, we used to . . ." He let it trail off, the gleam fading from his eyes even as she watched, her heart aching with the realization that he'd been thinking of Amanda and all he'd shared with her.

For what seemed an eternity, silence stretched like an abyss between them. Then Trevor shook his head, as though to clear it, before continuing, "I'm sorry. I have no right to pressure you this way, Diana. You have to do what's right for you. Meanwhile, why don't we finish up our plans for Christmas vacation so we can call Crystal?"

His abrupt change of mood was like a slap in the face even though she knew he was telling her exactly what she should want to hear. How could being her own person make her feel so lonely? She really hadn't wanted him to fight her decision to stay in Pleasant Valley, had she? It was frightening to realize just how confused she was.

TWELVE

Diana forced herself to stand at the airport window until the ATS Industries jet taxied away. She could feel the reality of Trevor's visit fading even before the plane hurled itself into the bright blue sky. The wonder and the joy they'd found in each other's arms yesterday afternoon took on a dreamlike quality when she contrasted it with the light kiss of farewell Trevor had dropped on her lips before he followed Harlan out the door.

But what had she expected? Trevor had retreated from the intimacy of her bed as soon as the call came. They'd spent the rest of the afternoon downstairs, acting as they had in the early days on the island. Friends, maybe that was all they could ever be. Anything else was far too dangerous, especially to Crystal.

Diana frowned as she drove back into town. There'd been an odd note in Crystal's voice when she heard that Trevor was in Pleasant Valley. Trevor hadn't noticed it, she was sure; but she knew her niece so well . . . Just not well enough to figure out what the coolness meant. Unless Crystal resented her for getting close to Trevor? The very thought made her shiver.

She couldn't think about it now, she told herself

firmly. In two hours she'd be meeting with Mr. Douglas and the Dahlmer sisters and she needed to be ready to bring up all the points that Trevor had suggested. Trevor. His image filled her mind and her heart and she couldn't stop the tears as she pulled into her garage. Right or wrong, she wished that she was on the jet with him, that she never had to be alone again. Christmas seemed a lifetime away.

Trevor made another tour of the house on Bellington Cay, checking each room carefully, seeking flaws or omissions. "You ain't missed a thing," Louise said from the kitchen door, her amused grin mocking him. "Place looks like a Christmas bazaar."

"You think I've overdone it?" He hated himself for the doubts that crowded around every time he had to make a decision.

"No more than the next man. They'll love it. Just give it a rest or you won't be around to welcome them tomorrow." Sympathy softened Louise's dark face, reminding him of how well she'd come to know him this last hectic week.

"I just want it to be perfect." He'd said that so often the words mocked him, but he couldn't seem to help himself. He wished mightily that Diana had agreed to fly out early with him; but even on the telephone, she'd seemed strangely distant since his visit to Pleasant Valley.

To his surprise, Louise frowned at him, instead of teasing him about his endless plans. "Nothing is perfect, Trevor. It's likely to rain some days and that daughter of yours is going to cause waves. Just be glad they're coming and let them enjoy their visit. And you enjoy it, too." Her dark eyes narrowed speculatively. "I wager, that's what Diana would tell you."

He winced, aware that Louise was probably right. "I wish she was here."

"I expect she does, too. She was most fond of the

sunshine, and according to the news, there's been little of that where she is.'' Louise's fond smile reminded him of how close Diana and his housekeeper had become. Louise had told him often enough how glad she was that Diana would be here for Christmas.

But would she just be visiting? That was the question that taunted him whenever he took the time to think about Diana. Was she just coming for Crystal's sake? Or did she want to be with him as much as he wanted her beside him? When he remembered their spectacular lovemaking, he was sure she shared his feelings; but her refusal to accept his invitations since worried him.

Was she afraid to get close to anyone because of the way her marriage had ended? But why couldn't she trust him? He'd done everything he could think of to let her know that he liked and respected her and that he wanted her to have a place in his life. Why did she keep running away?

He forced the doubts back as he went upstairs to his office, the only room in the house not overrun with Christmas decorations. He was going to win her over; it was just a matter of time. After all, he'd managed to convince her mother to trust him enough to come to the island for the holidays and he was definitely on the right track with Crystal.

He smiled as he sank down in his chair. He'd stopped by the Cliffton School for a visit with her before he flew to the island and the memories still warmed him. Crystal had made a point of introducing ''her father'' to hordes of giggling teenage girls and he'd loved every minute of it. Somehow, her introductions had given their relationship a legitimacy that nothing else could.

Well, he wasn't going to let Diana exit from his life after the holidays, so she'd just have to accept that fact—and find a way to trust him not to hurt her the way her ex-husband obviously had. Maybe if he could convince her to stay after Crystal and her mother flew back to the States . . .

The shrill of the telephone interrupted his erotic fantasies and he swallowed a sigh as Harlan began describing the latest twists and turns in the final merger negotiations. Though he still enjoyed the challenge of the business world, the complexity of his personal life was claiming a disturbing amount of his attention. It was something that had never happened while he was married to Amanda, no doubt because she'd been a part of both worlds.

"There is something here that might interest you, Trev," Harlan continued, forcing his mind back to the subject. "One of the properties we'll be getting in this merger is a small chain of bookstores in the Denver area. They've been badly mishandled, but according to the latest figures, they could be brought back by the right management." Harlan paused, then when Trevor said nothing, went on, "Say a manager with library training and maybe ideas on how to appeal to the younger generation?"

Trevor winced. So much for keeping his private life private from his best friend. Harlan was too good at reading people to have missed the clues he'd probably been dropping like red flags in the snow. He managed a chuckle to cover his frustration. "I think she's hoping for a teaching position, but I'd appreciate it if you'd send me the particulars in the next packet. Maybe this would appeal."

"I hope so. You'd be a lot more help if your brain was in Colorado full time instead of vacationing in Iowa." Harlan's tone was light, but his words confirmed Trevor's suspicions.

"A man has to do what he can for his family."

"Yeah." Harlan wisely moved on to other subjects.

"I don't believe any of this." Her mother's voice grated along Diana's already strained nerves like chalk on a blackboard. "Here I am flying off to the Caribbean like some kind of celebrity."

"I could get used to it." Crystal stretched like a golden cat and grinned at them both. "Jennifer was positively green when Trevor came to visit."

Diana cast a quick glance at her mother, hoping that she wasn't going to start lecturing Crystal about her values, and was relieved to see that she was smiling. Obviously, Sarah Johnson had decided to keep an open mind where Trevor Sinclair was concerned, which, under the circumstances, was the best Diana could hope for.

Diana shifted nervously and peered out the window. Not that she could see anything but clouds below the sleek jet, but she was finding it harder and harder to endure her family's curious glances. She felt as though they could read the confusion on her face, but whenever she thought of Trevor, she was torn by her doubts and her unbearable longing to be near him. That fact made the upcoming visit to the island either a dream come true or the biggest mistake she'd ever make.

Unable to sit still, she got up to refill her coffee cup. If only she knew how he felt, whether his desire for her came from his heart or was just a sign that he was returning to life. Could he ever love her? Or was he just hoping to re-create the woman he'd lost? She swallowed a sigh. Her marriage had been anything but happy, yet it had left her with far fewer problems when it came to moving on. No man would ever have to live up to a standard set by Ken Foster.

"So what else did Trevor tell you about his plans?" her mother was asking Crystal. "I mean, what is there to do on this island?"

Diana closed her eyes, not hearing Crystal's eager answer. She was lost in images of walks on the beach, of moonlit nights and magical kisses. She and Trevor had laughed in the sunlight and dreamed as they explored the coastline in his boat, and somewhere during those lovely days and special nights, she'd lost her heart. The question was, could she ever reclaim it, even if she wanted to?

Trevor watched as the jet circled, then came in for another of Sam's perfect landings. A light breeze had herded the morning storm clouds away and late afternoon sunshine sparkled on the waves that washed the far end of the landing strip. Once Sam cut power, the silence was deafening; Trevor was the only one waiting, since Belle, Sam's girlfriend, had merely left her old pickup parked by the landing strip and walked back home nearly an hour ago.

Heart pounding with anticipation, Trevor hurried forward as the door opened and his guests prepared to descend. Somehow he wasn't surprised when Crystal was the first off, but her excited hug made his long, lonely wait worthwhile. "Where is everybody?" she demanded, looking around.

"The brass band was booked, but according to Louise, most of the teenagers are soaking up rays at Sandy Point." He teased her without worrying, far more comfortable with her now than he'd thought possible when he put her on the plane home after her Thanksgiving visit.

"I suppose it's too late for me to join them today." Crystal sighed. "My tan really faded at school."

"You'll have plenty of time to work on it tomorrow," he promised, but his attention was already on the woman emerging from the plane. She took his breath away, literally.

Just looking at Diana as the breeze tugged at her tawny mane and stirred her proper skirt to display an extra few inches of her incredible legs was enough to tell him that nothing had changed in his feelings for her. She was so special, so exciting, he wanted to run to her and pull her into his arms. He wanted to kiss her until all her doubts and reservations disappeared, but that was impossible. She was too damned busy helping her mother with what looked like a dozen bags of gaily wrapped packages.

He caught his breath and hurried to assist them both, aware that just touching Diana's arm wasn't going to be enough to satisfy the screaming need inside him, but willing to settle for it—for the moment. When she looked up at him, he recognized the flaring heat in the depths of her eyes and his body tightened in response. It was, he realized, going to be a long and difficult ten days; but at least she was finally here.

Diana was grateful for Crystal's excited babble as they made the short drive from the airstrip to the house. Just seeing Trevor had confirmed her worst fears—nothing had changed. She still ached to be in his arms and hungered for his kisses and his touch. The thought of occupying the same house with him and pretending that she didn't want him promised exquisite torment. Yet there was no other place on earth she wanted to be.

The days before Christmas were both better than she'd dared hope and more painful. Thanks to Trevor's careful planning, everything moved with surprising ease. As she watched, he charmed her mother, telling her stories about Eileen's short college career, making her laugh in a way Diana hadn't heard in a long time. And where Crystal was concerned, she could only marvel at his casual ease.

At first, she was happy for him, pleased that all his hard work had paid off. But as the days skipped by, busy and fun though they were, she began to realize something. Trevor no longer needed her. Her mother had accepted his right to be a part of Crystal's life and Crystal was glorying in his attention. The house rang with her giggles as she responded to his teasing with her own quick thrusts of wit, as comfortable with him as though she'd always had a father.

Diana stood in the kitchen doorway taking a break from helping Louise with the final preparations for the Christmas Eve dinner that had been scenting the house for hours. Trevor and Crystal were on the floor in front of the huge Christmas tree that dominated one corner of the room. As she watched, Crystal began shaking the various packages, guessing at the contents and sending Trevor into gales of laughter at her outrageous suggestions. Sarah, on the couch in front of the fire, was observing them, too, and laughing.

" 'Tis what he's been needing.'' Louise spoke softly. "He's a man meant for family, though he's not had much chance, poor soul, what with his wife being taken so young. You brought him a rich gift, Diana.''

"They needed each other.'' She spoke quickly, keeping her head turned so that Louise wouldn't see the tears she couldn't blink back. A shameful jealousy struck her as she stood on the outside, seeing their joy, aching to be a part of it, yet no longer needed by any of them. She swallowed a sob. "I'll check the table.''

The dining room was dim, so she could hide there as she did her best to mop away her unwanted tears. What kind of person would begrudge Trevor and Crystal and even her mother the happiness they were sharing? Their pleasure took nothing from her . . . except the dream to which she had no right. She closed her eyes tight, fighting back a fresh wash of self-pity.

"Diana.'' His voice was so soft that for a moment she thought she might have imagined it; then she felt his hands on her shoulders, caressing, gentle, as he turned her to face him. "Why are you hiding in here?''

His fingers forced her head up so she had no hope of hiding the ravages of her tears. She drew in a shaky breath, wishing that she could answer him, but she was beyond speech. His frown echoed the concern in his voice and she shivered as he gently wiped his thumbs over the damp trails on her cheeks.

"What is it? Has something happened to hurt you? Tell me please. Let me make it right. I want this to be the happiest Christmas ever for you, too. Don't you know that?''

For a heartbeat, she wanted to tell him how she felt, how much she'd come to love him, but she couldn't. To tell him now would only make it worse, since he obviously didn't return her feelings. She couldn't ruin his holiday by making him feel guilty over breaking her heart.

Slowly, painfully, she managed to produce a shaky smile. "Just a little Christmas melancholy. Everything that's happened today reminds me of some lonely Christmases we have spent. Then I looked in and thought about Daddy and Eileen and wished that they could have been here to see how happy you've made my family."

"You're my family, too. And I can understand your feelings. Believe me, my last few Christmases were pretty bleak. Having a family makes all the difference." His hands cupped her face as he sought her lips, touching them lightly at first; then suddenly his arms slipped around her, pulling her close as he deepened the kiss.

A shudder of pure desire shattered her fragile control as she answered his hunger with her own, telling him with her kiss what she dared not put into words. The emptiness she'd felt burned away when she was in his arms and, for that moment, nothing else mattered.

"Hey, Louise, when's dinner going to be ready?" Crystal's voice came from close at hand, destroying the illusion of privacy.

Diana pulled away, her breath coming in sobs as she looked up at Trevor, shocked by the return of sanity. Her hand shook as she tried to smooth her hair back into place. He appeared as dazed as she felt.

"Where is everybody, anyway?" Crystal asked, emerging from the kitchen with a stalk of celery in her hand. "We're never going to get to the presents if we don't eat."

Trevor caught Diana's hand and gave it a quick squeeze, then stepped forward, leaving her in the shadowy corner where he'd found her. "Considering what you told me you thought was in those boxes, Crystal, I don't see why you're so eager to open them."

"You don't think I expect to be right, do you?" Crystal's giggle trailed behind her as Trevor followed her back into the living room, leaving Diana to recover in private.

Diana leaned against the wall, her knees still a little weak. Did he mean it—the kiss and his words about her being his family, too? She wanted to believe it was possible; she had to if she was to survive the remaining days here. His kiss had to mean something.

So she'd give it a try. Thanks to her mother and Crystal's constant company, she knew Trevor wouldn't be able to say anything or do more than steal an occasional kiss; but if they were together . . . Hope blossomed through her, lifting her spirits, reviving the dreams that filled her days and nights. Maybe, just this once, she'd take a chance. If Trevor could love her, nothing else would matter.

From that moment on, her life took on a magical quality. Every glance, every touch seemed to have a special meaning and the aura of romance cloaked them whenever they could steal a few minutes alone. Even the secrecy they felt they must maintain for Crystal's sake added to the fun. It was exciting to slip away and meet for a few frenzied kisses, to be forced apart by the sound of approaching footsteps.

The days and nights raced by. She gloried in Trevor's embrace as they danced on the dinner cruise; she shivered as he pressed his heated body to hers when they passed in the upper hall. Even looking into his eyes made her heartbeat quicken, for she could see the echoing flame there.

They had just three days left before New Year's Eve when the call came. Since Diana was helping Louise with the luncheon preparations, she answered the kitchen phone. A chill of premonition chased down her spine as soon as her aunt asked to speak to Sarah. Still, there was nothing she could do but hand the receiver to her mother and wait, hoping that nothing had happened in Phoenix that would spoil this special time.

Her mother's smile became a frown as she listened, but she looked to Trevor, not Diana, after she hung up the receiver. "Is there any way I can get on a flight to Phoenix tomorrow?"

"I can make a call and find out. Why? Is there something wrong?" Trevor asked.

"It's my doctor appointment. I forgot to change it, and when Betty called, he told her that he's going to be out of town for a month." She sighed, looking worried and unhappy for the first time in days. "I could see someone else, I suppose, but he's the only one who has been able to help me and he said he'd work me in if I could get back by day after tomorrow."

"Then you will." Trevor patted her shoulder as he went to the phone. "Let me check the airlines. I'd use the corporate jet, but Sam's already halfway to California, so it would be hard to get him back in time to . . ." He began punching in numbers.

It took several calls, but Diana wasn't surprised when Trevor announced as they sat down to lunch that everything was settled. They would fly to Nassau with her mother tomorrow morning and she'd be home in Phoenix in time for dinner.

Only Crystal greeted the news with a frown. "Do I have to go? We're supposed to go out exploring tomorrow. Benj claims he knows where there's a pirate cave that might have some old gold coins hidden in it."

Louise chuckled from her place at the sink. "Ben Hoffman has been sifting the sand in that cave since he was knee high and I don't recall a single coin turning up."

Trevor gave Diana a questioning glance, then turned to Crystal. "I guess you really don't have to come, if you don't want to, Crystal. But the three of us could do some shopping in Nassau before we catch the flight back.''

Crystal considered for a moment, then shook her head. ''You guys go ahead and shop. If I find a pirate's treasure, I'll buy Nassau.''

Diana chuckled. ''Guess the Straw Market can't compete with a genuine pirate cave.''

''So we won't even try.'' Trevor's gaze turned the food in her mouth to sawdust and robbed her of breath. It was several seconds before she even remembered how to chew and swallow. Luckily, her mother was so busy fussing about all she had to do to be ready, no one else seemed to notice the rise in the room temperature.

Though she managed to get her wayward emotions back under control, the rest of the day passed in a haze of anticipation. Finally, she and Trevor would have some time alone, a chance to talk. They'd have four hours in Nassau after her mother's flight left and, of course, there was the forced intimacy of the flight back to Bellington Cay. Every time she thought about it, her pulse rate jumped wildly.

What would he say? Would they finally talk about the future in a way that included their feelings for each other? Or was she still living in a dream world, making plans that could never come true? Everything had been so wonderful since their blazing kiss in the dining room, but she couldn't be sure what that meant.

Trevor wanted her, but what if that was all? Could she bear it if he simply saw her as someone to enjoy and make love with for the moment? A chill chased down her spine as she remembered the nights when she'd stood outside Eileen's room and listened to her sister's heartbroken sobs.

She couldn't blame Trevor since she'd never asked for a commitment; there was no way he could know how she felt. She'd given herself to him wholeheartedly each time they'd made love, which meant he could believe that making love meant no more to her than it did to him. And how much had it meant to him? That was the question that tormented her as she lay in her twin bed and listened to Crystal's soft breathing through the night.

What if they made love again and then he told her that it had to be the last time, that it wasn't right for them to be involved because of Crystal? Or because he was still grieving for his perfect Amanda. Or because she simply wasn't right for him. All those possibilities existed and it frightened her to think about them; yet she had to, had to prepare herself just in case she was heading for heartbreak instead of joy.

The day dawned cloudy, but the breeze was already chasing the clouds away as the interisland flight took off. Diana sat beside her mother on the small plane, but her thoughts were focused on the man across the aisle. Though she usually had no trouble reading Trevor's moods, he seemed unusually quiet today and that made her nervous.

"You know, you two really didn't have to come with me, Diana," her mother said, forcing her attention back to their side of the narrow aisle. "I'm perfectly capable of catching the right plane."

"I think Trevor felt bad about not having the jet available. Besides, you haven't seen the chaos at the airport during the holidays." Diana felt a little uncomfortable under her mother's narrowed gaze, but she managed a smile.

"I suspect you both would like a little time alone." Her mother arched an eyebrow at her. "Family is wonderful, but I've spent enough time as a guest in Betty and Fred's home to know that everybody needs a breather from time to time."

Guilt paralyzed her throat as she met her mother's gaze for a moment, then quickly looked away. Mom couldn't know! She and Trevor had been so careful, so casual with each other whenever they weren't alone. She tried to think of something to say to end the terrible silence stretching between them, but her brain refused to work.

"I'm not going to pry, Diana; but I just want you to remember what happened to Eileen when she got mixed up with Trevor. He's a wonderful and charming man, but so was Ken Foster—at least on the surface. Yet your marriage turned out to be a disaster for you. You're on the rebound and so, I suspect, is Trevor. Just remember that and be careful, okay?"

"He's nothing like Ken." That was all she could say. Any other denial would have to be a lie, for it was already far too late to be careful with her heart.

Her mother said nothing more; but for the rest of the flight and up until the moment she waved goodbye and boarded the big jet, Diana was conscious of her worried glances. They definitely cast a pall over what she'd hoped would be a perfect interlude with Trevor.

Trevor caught her hand as she let it drop to her side. "So, do you really want to go shopping?" His grin was properly wicked when she turned to him.

It took her a moment to catch her breath enough to ask, "Why whatever do you have in mind, Mr. Sinclair?"

"Actually, I was going to suggest that we take the rental car, pick up some food for a picnic, then explore the less populous areas of this island. I've heard there are some truly beautiful places so well hidden that only the islanders know about them."

"Finding them should be a lovely challenge." Her heart was pounding so hard, she wondered why the people crowding the airport weren't all staring at her.

His eyes flickered with green fire, warming her like a caress as he led her through the crowd and out into the fresh air. Mom had to be wrong. He was over Amanda and she'd all but forgotten Ken. This wasn't rebound; it was magic. She sat close to him in the car, her hand resting on his muscular thigh, glorying in the play of his muscles as he drove.

"Do you know where we're going?" she asked when her vision cleared enough to look out the window at what appeared to be an untamed tropical jungle.

"Floyd told me about a small waterfall out here somewhere. He said it was very special." He covered her hand with his, pressing her fingers into his hard flesh so that she could feel the blazing heat of his need for her. "And very private."

Trevor caught his breath as he watched her swallow and saw the heat rising in her cheeks—not a blush but a glowing that reflected the fiery passion he knew burned inside her. It was the passion he meant to lose himself in, just as soon as he found the blasted waterfall that Floyd had described.

The car bucked and shimmied slightly as the track he'd been following grew even rougher. If he'd chosen the wrong turnoff, he was going to have a hell of a time getting out of here, he realized; then the road turned around a thick growth of oleander and ended— at a beautiful little pool fed by the silvery splashing of a tiny, but perfect waterfall.

Relief swept through him as he hit the brakes, then shut off the motor. The silence was like warm honey as it surrounded them. "Welcome to paradise," he whispered as he pulled her into his arms.

It was several wonderously passionate minutes before he released her lips long enough so the two of them could get out of the car. Diana looked around, her expression slightly dazed. "It is paradise," she murmured. "It's like our own private world."

"Which we need." He reached for her again, pulling her hard against his aching body. "I love having family around, but I don't know how much longer . . ." He let the words trail off as he plundered her mouth.

Her lips told him that she shared his frustration, as well as his delight in escaping. Though he'd wanted to talk first, to explain about the job and discuss her future, nothing mattered but her mouth opening beneath his, her body responding wildly to his touch, her desire blazing to meet his as they both settled to the slightly damp grass, so completely entwined that he was no longer sure where he ended and Diana began.

For Diana, surrender came quickly, wonderfully, as they soared together, reveling in their loving union; finding that perfect place where they were one and nothing and no one else existed. Love washed away her doubts and fears and left only the magic, the joy— Trevor.

She lay spent in his arms, the crescendo of love ebbing into a sweet satisfaction. She felt so safe, so loved and cared for, it was hard to think of anything beyond this perfect moment and the tender lassitude that made his chest the ideal pillow, his heartbeat a lullaby.

Trevor shifted slightly, cradling her softness close to keep from disturbing her. He wanted this total oneness to last forever, for he remembered too clearly the emptiness that had followed whenever he let Diana out of his arms. Right or wrong, he had to find a way to keep her at his side. But how? He closed his eyes, letting his mind drift, hoping that in this wonderful moment of fulfillment, he'd find the secret, the key to her barricaded heart.

It was cold. Diana shifted slightly, snuggling closer to the warmth beside her, wondering why the covers weren't protecting her from the icy feel of the wind. Had she left the window open or . . .

The source of warmth groaned and strong arms suddenly tightened around her. Reality brought her eyes open and, at the same time, her memory returned, banishing her dream world. Gulping, she eased away from Trevor and tried to sit up. The wind sent shivers through her and brought up the gooseflesh on her naked skin. The fickle sun had vanished beneath the threatening clouds now gathering above them.

Trevor opened his eyes, then grinned at her, his gaze caressing her until he looked beyond her shoulders to the sky. "Oh, oh." He frowned as he sat up. "I think we'd better get in the car now."

The next few moments were spent grabbing for their clothes and awkwardly donning them as they hurried to the car. They'd barely made it inside when the sky seemed to split above them and sheets of rain swept over the tiny clearing, hiding everything.

"Guess this means our picnic is going to have to be in the car," Diana observed, finding it hard to be upset while her body still glowed with the memory of his touch.

"I hope that's our only problem." Trevor was looking at his watch.

"What do you mean?" Diana looked up from the sacks of food they'd abandoned earlier.

"The road in wasn't that great. If the rain is heavy, we could end up stuck out here for a while. Did you know we slept over an hour?"

"Are you saying we could miss our plane." The chill she'd felt earlier returned, though it was warm in the car.

"They might not even be flying. The flights get canceled if the rain squalls are extensive. Anyway, I think I'd better try driving out of here now before the ground has a chance to soak up too much water." He started the car.

By the time they finally emerged from the meandering back road, Diana felt as though she'd personally pushed and pulled the slithering car along the muddy road and Trevor's face was gray from the strain. "Are we going to make it back in time?" she asked as they moved along the main road.

Trevor shrugged. "I think there's a small café up ahead and I expect they have a telephone. We can call the airport from there."

He looked so worried, Diana said nothing else. Guilt

swept through her. What had they done? And what would happen if their stolen moments made them miss the plane? How could they ever face Crystal? Or themselves?

THIRTEEN

Diana sat at the counter, warming her hands on the mug of coffee she'd ordered as she waited for Trevor, who'd followed the waiter into a short hallway on the other side of the small café. She checked her watch again, unwilling to believe that so much time had passed since her mother's plane left. If her watch was right, they had about fifteen minutes to make the return flight to Bellington Cay.

She shifted on the stool. So where was Trevor? He'd had time enough to call six airports. His coffee would be stone cold by the time he got back. She closed her eyes, well aware that cold coffee wasn't what was worrying her. A sound from across the room snapped her eyes open.

Trevor's grin reached out to her like a friendly caress and relief warmed her as the coffee hadn't. "Has the flight been delayed by the storm?" she asked as he slid onto the stool beside her.

Trevor shook his head. "It's been canceled. In fact, no planes have taken off for the last hour and a half. According to the weather reports, the storm is pretty general and is expected to last the rest of the day and into the night. We're stranded."

His expression hadn't changed. If anything, he looked even happier about it. Diana shook her head, suddenly wondering if she was still dreaming. His carefree attitude made no sense at all. "You mean we can't get back?"

He chuckled. "I called Louise and asked her to stay at the house with Crystal tonight. She said everyone's fine there. In fact, they were worried about us, afraid that we might take off not realizing how bad the storm was." His gaze met hers with smoldering force, his lazy grin fading. "It looks like we'll just have to amuse ourselves for the rest of the day . . . and night."

"Oh." Her throat was suddenly dry as realization burned through her. "But where . . . ?"

"That's what took me so long. I tried calling a couple of the resorts, but everything is full because of the holidays. Luckily, Floyd McMurtry's guest house is still available. Otherwise we might have to sleep in the car—or beside it." The wicked gleam in his eyes told her that he was reliving what had happened before their earlier nap.

Was she blushing? Her cheeks felt warm, but not nearly so hot as the rest of her. A soft chuckle rose in her throat and she found herself smiling. "In that case, perhaps we should order something to eat. We can save our picnic for later, in front of the fire . . ."

"Much, much later." His low whisper and heated gaze curled around her like a lover's embrace and it was several seconds before either of them noticed the waitress patiently waiting to take their order.

The rain was still pouring down when Trevor edged the rented car as close as possible to the guest house door. He leaned back with a sigh. "This has got to be the worst cloudburst I've ever seen here. I'm glad Ben insisted on cutting the cave explorations short; some of those are pretty close to the tide line and with the wind . . ."

"Crystal is all right?" Diana frowned at the images his words evoked.

"I could hear rock music blasting and what sounded like a dozen kids talking in the background. We're going to owe Louise big time for this." He didn't look worried about the debt. "Are you ready to go in?"

Her heartbeat quickened as he began gathering the sacks of food, then handed them to her before he eased his door open. "Wait here until I get the door unlocked," he advised, before he slid out and raced to the meager shelter of the front porch. Once there, he spent several minutes feeling around beneath the dripping eaves until he located the key hidden there.

Diana took a deep breath, then hurried after him, doing her best to shelter the sacks under her already wet sweater. She was dripping by the time she stepped into the cold, damp main room of the cottage. Trevor grinned at her from the hearth where he was already putting a match to the fire that had been laid there.

"Floyd said we should help ourselves to the dry clothes hanging in the closets and we're welcome to anything we can find in the cupboards or refrigerator. He always keeps the place ready for anyone who might need it."

"He's a good friend to have."

"He sure is; he's the one who told me about the waterfall."

Since she couldn't think of anything to say to that, Diana headed for one of the bedrooms that opened off the main room. A search of the closet yielded three bathing suits, a terry robe, and a rather tired looking navy sweatsuit that seemed about her size. Shivering, she stripped off all her clothes and hung them in the bathroom, then toweled herself dry before pulling on the sweatsuit.

The mirror told her that she still resembled a drowned puppy, but at least she felt warmer. Of course, a little glass of wine or brandy would help even more. With that in mind, she slipped her feet into a pair of thong sandals and padded out to see what Trevor had found.

"Took you long enough," he teased, patting the couch beside him as he poured brandy into a glass. "All warm again?" He looked quite dashing in a bright red sweatsuit, his hair still tousled from the toweling he'd given it.

"I'm feeling much better, thank you." She snuggled against him, enjoying the feel of his arm around her as she stared into the flames that were now warming the room.

"Comfortable enough to talk?"

"About what?" She really didn't care whether they talked at all; just being here with him was heavenly. For all she cared it could rain forever.

"The future." The note of seriousness in his voice broke through her growing contentment.

Diana stilled, not even breathing for a moment. Hope and doubt warred inside her, making her afraid to speak or even look at him. What if he'd changed his mind? What if he'd begun to realize that making love with her was a mistake and . . . She swallowed hard, forcing back her fears. "What about the future?"

"Well, I know you're still having trouble finding a teaching position and it just so happens that I've found something that might interest you. Actually, I should say it found me—we took over the property as a part of the merger Harlan and I have been working on."

She slanted a glance in his direction, hoping for a clue to what he was talking about, but his attention seemed to be focused on the blazing log. Her courage wavered, but she couldn't turn back. It was far too late and there was nowhere for her heart to run. Unfortunately, she couldn't speak around the lump in her throat, not even to refuse his help.

"It's a chain of bookstores, in Denver. Three of them, all in pretty fair locations. The stats are good on them, though they've been badly mishandled. That's where you come in. With your background, you should be able to get them back on their feet.''

He stopped speaking again, obviously expecting her to say something, but no words came. Bookstores in Denver? Though she'd sworn to be independent, the idea was tempting, especially since she'd had no luck job hunting on her own. Besides, in Denver she'd be close to Trevor.

Trevor shifted slightly and she could feel the tension of the arm that still rested on her shoulders. ''I know it isn't exactly what you want, Diana, but it is a good deal. You could try it for a while. I just know you'd like running your own business and I'd be glad to help you, if you ran into any problems. Besides, if you took it, you'd be in Denver and we could be together all the time.''

He paused again, then slowly turned to meet her gaze. His frown sent a chill through her. She had to say something, but what? Though a part of her wanted to accept his offer, a warning voice screamed that it would be a mistake, that it was just the first step. Once she accepted, she'd never be free again. He was so strong, so sure that he was right and she . . . She loved him far too much to protect herself.

''Say something, Diana. Don't you think it's a great idea? I know the two of us can make it work. Besides, think how wonderful it would be for Crystal. We'd be able to . . .''

The mention of Crystal did it. The warning voice became a siren, screaming that Crystal was his reason for finding her the job, for wanting her close. He saw them as a package deal. The pain was more than she could bear!

Diana jumped to her feet, away from his arm, fleeing the tender power of his touch; but she couldn't escape his gaze. Though she didn't want to, she could see the hurt and confusion there. For a moment, she considered explaining, but she couldn't. To do so would bare a part of her soul that no one had ever seen. She was trapped between his pain and her love.

"Diana, what is it?" He started to get up.

She backed away from him, feeling the room closing around her. If he took her in his arms now, she'd be lost. And all of their lives would be destroyed. Grasping at straws, she gave him the only excuse she could think of. "I can't, Trevor. I don't belong in Denver or in a bookstore. I don't want to be a businesswoman. I want to teach. I need to be free."

He didn't even seem to hear her. "You need me, Diana. Today, the past few days prove that. We've been happy and close and I can't let you go. I need you and I'll take care of you. You don't have to be afraid. If you don't want to run the bookstores, we'll find something else, but . . ."

She didn't stay to listen to any more. Oblivious to the rain, she raced out the door and ran along the beach. Being cold and wet was better than surrendering to her own aching heart. Escape was all that could save her from losing herself completely to a man who could never love her as she really was.

Trevor was too stunned to move for several minutes. Even as he watched Diana, reading the genuine pain and horror in her face, he couldn't believe it was happening, and when she ran out, he just watched the door as it slammed back against the side of the cottage, caught in the wind. The cold slash of wet air finally broke through his trance and he hurried after her, shouting her name and wondering what the hell he had done to cause this reaction.

Running in the thongs was awkward at best and fighting the rain and wind made it even worse, slowing her strides as soon as she was clear of the house. She heard him calling to her even over the thunder of the waves and felt her heart breaking, but she forced herself to keep moving. For all their sakes, it had to end here and now before they destroyed each other and Crystal.

For a moment images of their closeness during the past days filled her mind, deepening the pain with the reflection of joy. Sobs rose in her throat and warm tears joined the cold rain on her cheeks. If only he'd been able to love her; if only he'd seen the real Diana instead of a substitute for his lost Amanda or a mother for Crystal. If only . . .

She tried to move faster, not even looking back to see if he was following. It didn't matter where she went, only that she went alone. Somehow she had to find the independence she'd lost during her marriage; somehow she must regain the strength and purpose and resolve . . .

Her foot caught in something, her ankle twisting as she went sprawling on the soaking sand. Stunned by the impact, she lay there an eternity before she could catch her breath enough to sob out her heartbreak and frustration. She knew even before she tried to get up that she wouldn't be able to run any farther; the throbbing pain made it difficult to even stand.

What was she going to do? Shivers chased over her, the soaked fabric offering no protection against the wind or the cold. The guest house had vanished behind the bushes and trees that grew along the curving beach and no light relieved the darkness. For just a heartbeat, she considered simply lying back down and waiting for the waves; then she shook back her streaming hair and squinted through the rain.

Ahead a square shape appeared and disappeared as the trees and bushes bent to the wind's will. Gritting her teeth, she hobbled toward it, praying that it was more than a shadowy illusion born of her desperation. She nearly collapsed with relief when she encountered the wet wooden wall. Leaning most of her weight on it, she felt her way along until she found the door. It opened easily and she stumbled inside, too exhausted to take another step.

It was cold and dark but dry, and when she crawled

away from the door, she found what felt like a pile of canvas fabric. With the last of her strength, she rolled herself up in the musty folds and closed her eyes, trying to escape the nightmare that her life had become.

Where the devil was she? Trevor stopped again, trying to peer through the steadily worsening downpour. Had she doubled back? He'd lost sight of her when she rounded the point, and now the beach stretched ahead, empty of life. He shivered, feeling the cold since he'd stopped running.

Should he go back? A part of his mind told him he might as well, but he couldn't. Every time he closed his eyes, he saw her face with that stricken expression and he knew that, somehow, it was his fault. He couldn't bear it. He had to find her and let her know that . . .

He kicked something as he started forward again and stopped to pick it up. A thong sandal and beside it lay a snaking vine half torn from the ground. Had Diana fallen? Did this mean she was now barefoot and possibly injured? He looked around again, then headed away from the beach at a jog. The old storage shack was around here somewhere—the one where Floyd kept his sailing gear so it would be handy to the little dock that extended out just the other side of the rocks.

The creaking of the door penetrated the cold fog that seemed to surround her. Diana stiffened, trying to still her chattering teeth so she could hear more, but the storm was too noisy. She huddled, afraid of being found, but suddenly even more afraid of the lonely abyss that seemed to stretch ahead of her.

"Diana, are you in here?" Trevor's voice seemed to come from so close she couldn't keep back a whimper of surprise.

"Where are you? I don't want to step on you." He cursed softly. "I wish I still smoked. At least that way I'd have a match to light. Maybe Floyd left some . . ."

The shuffling sounds began and she forced herself to sit up. "I'm over here, Trevor."

"Aha!" The movement stopped and in a moment a pinpoint of light flared, nearly blinding her. "Now if there's just fuel in this lantern . . ."

He cursed and shook the match out as it burned his fingers, then lit another. In a moment soft light bloomed from the old-fashioned lantern. Trevor held it high and looked at her, frowning. "What in the world have you done to yourself, Diana?" he demanded, coming over to kneel beside her. "You're covered with mud and sand. And is that blood on your cheek?"

His touch was so gentle, so tender that it shattered her heart beyond repair. She tried to answer, but only sobs filled her throat, and when he drew her into his arms, no words were necessary. For now it was enough that he was here, that she was safe in his embrace.

As her sobs slowed, her doubts returned; but this time she couldn't escape. And she didn't want to. She shivered at the thought and the weakness of character it betrayed.

"We should be getting back. You're freezing." Trevor shifted slightly, trying to draw the sail fabric more closely around her.

Protests rose in her mind. So long as they were trapped here together, she could cling to him, could feel his wonderful closeness; once they returned to the guest house, she'd have to find another way to leave. "I can't walk. I fell and I think I've sprained my ankle."

"I'll carry you."

"It's too far and the storm is getting worse. At least we have shelter here."

Trevor hesitated, sensing another reason behind her words. But what could it be? Why would she want to stay in a cold, dark shack when there was a nice warm house . . . She snuggled closer against his side and he realized that he didn't care. If she was content to wait out the storm here, so was he.

"If we're going to stay, I think we should conserve our fuel," he said, reaching out to turn off the lantern. "I don't think there's more than an hour's worth in there."

Another shiver traced through her, but Diana knew it wasn't from the cold. She was feeling warmer with every passing second. Just being in Trevor's arms was worth the discomfort of wet clothes and a throbbing ankle. The silence between them lengthened, but she felt no discomfort, only joy at the enforced intimacy as the darkness wrapped itself around them and held them close.

Trevor stirred, painfully aware of his growing desire. Just holding her in his arms wasn't going to be enough for much longer; yet he hesitated to take advantage of the situation. How could he make love to her after she'd run away from him? Sharing sexual fulfillment wasn't enough for him, not anymore. He wanted all of her and if she wasn't willing to give it . . .

He tightened his embrace and took the plunge. "Why don't you tell me why we're here, Diana?"

"What . . ." She stiffened in his arms and he had a horrible feeling that she was once again wearing that stricken expression.

"Why did you run away from me? All I wanted was to help you through a difficult time in your life. You acted as though I wanted to . . . to imprison you."

For a moment she considered denying his words, but she couldn't lie to him—or to herself. Knowing it would end even this stolen moment, she answered him. "Don't you? Aren't you trying to make me into someone I'm not, someone who would suit you better than a small-town teacher?"

"What?" His arms loosened, just as she'd expected, but his hands bit into her arms as he faced her in the darkness. "Is that what you thought I was doing? But why? Why do you think I want to change you? Have I ever said anything to make you think such a thing?''

''Every time you mention a job, it's in business.'' Though her answer came quickly, even she could hear the lack of conviction in her voice. ''It's as though you want me to be a part of your world like . . .'' She couldn't finish the sentence.

The silence throbbed and deepened as she waited, her head whirling with confusion. Could she have been wrong? But every single thing he said had seemed so familiar, so like the way Ken had ''suggested'' improvements to her.

''Didn't it ever occur to you that I offered business positions because those were the only positions I had to offer you?'' The hurt was evident in his voice, and when he let her go, she felt as though the bottom had dropped out of her world.

Shame swept over her and fresh tears burned in her eyes. How could she have misjudged him? How could she have thought that he'd be anything like Ken? She felt his pain and hated herself for having inflicted it.

''Why didn't you trust me, Diana?''

The sorrow in his voice stripped away her need to hide her feelings. No matter how vulnerable it made her, she couldn't leave him hurting; she loved him far too much. Slowly, painfully, she began to describe her life with Ken Foster, hiding nothing, not even the aching void that was left now that she'd lost Trevor's love.

It seemed to take forever, but finally it was all said. The whole ugly story lay between them. She shivered, wishing that he'd left the lantern burning so that she could see his face, could see if she'd managed to blunt the hurt she'd caused. But there was only the darkness and the stillness between them that seemed even deeper because of the storm outside.

Trevor shifted on the hard floor and drew in a slow breath, seeking inside himself for the right words. Never had he guessed how vulnerable Diana was. Her courage had fooled him from the moment they met and now her honesty humbled him. He wondered if he could match it and if that would be enough. All he knew was that he had to try.

"I don't want another Amanda in my life, Diana. What we had was incredible and special, but I'm a different man now. The young man who loved her is gone forever, as is she. When I lost her, I was sure that I could never love again. I didn't even want to try. That changed the evening you came into the Jolly Roger." He paused, hoping for some sign that she was willing to listen, but there was nothing to hear but the howling wind and pounding waves.

"You brought me back to life by telling me that I had someone to live for—a daughter. I told myself that would be enough, that getting to know Crystal and winning her love were all that mattered. And at first I believed that."

He felt rather than heard her sharp intake of breath and knew that he'd touched another sore spot. "But it wasn't nearly enough. I love Crystal, but she's almost a young woman now and she won't need me for very long. She couldn't fill the void inside me. That's what being around you taught me—being half alive wasn't going to be enough for me. When I held you, when I kissed you and you answered with such fire . . . After that night at Hibiscus Cove I knew I wanted you for yourself, that it had nothing to do with Crystal or loneliness or any of the other reasons I'd come up with and that scared me to death. All I could think about was the risk, the pain that love could bring."

Love! She was afraid to believe he meant it, yet just hearing him say the word was enough for her to reach out to him, finding his hand in the darkness. Lacing her fingers through his seemed so right, and she desperately needed something to hold on to now that hope had once more put her world into a spin.

"I tried to deny my feelings. I tried to ignore them,

but they didn't go away. I didn't mean to push you; I knew that you'd been hurt by your ex-husband. I just had no idea how badly. Knowing that you needed time was the reason I kept trying to come up with job ideas that would bring you to Denver. I thought maybe if we spent more time together, just dating instead of trying to work things out with your mother and Crystal . . .''

He drew her slowly to him, his touch gentle as he released her hand and wrapped his arms around her. ''I wanted to protect you while you were healing and all I did was make the wounds deeper. I'm sorry.''

For a moment it was enough just to be held, to feel his love surrounding her; then she lifted her head from his chest. ''Can you forgive me for not trusting you, Trevor? You've given me nothing but kindness and love and I still ran away. I was just so afraid of disappointing you the way I disappointed Ken. I was never quite right about anything and after a while . . .''

His mouth stopped her words, his lips gently teasing at first, then as she answered, his kiss became demanding and hungry. Once again, she felt her heart shattering inside her, but this time it was the ice of doubt falling away as she opened herself to him completely.

''I love you, Diana Johnson Foster, teacher, small-town girl. You're the perfect woman for me. You could only disappoint me by not loving me. I want to share my life with you and to have you share your life with me. Will you?'' His breath warmed her ear as he nibbled kisses on the tender skin of her neck.

''I've never wanted anything more.'' She said the words without thinking, glorying in the vulnerability she offered him. She felt the relief that shuddered through him as she slipped her hands beneath his soggy sweatshirt to caress his hard-muscled back. She pulled him closer, holding onto him with all the need and hunger and longing she'd never dared to show before.

As his kisses ignited the flames inside her, she realized that she'd never truly made love before. This time his caresses were echoed within the depths of her soul, and each touch banished her doubts and fears and cleansed away the ugliness of the past. The pure fire of her love grew and blossomed, filling her so that when they rose to the passionate crest of their joy, it was all giving and healing and taking and melding into the ecstacy of boundless love.

Much later, when she drifted back from paradise to the reality of the shack, Trevor sighed and sat up. "It sounds like the storm is about over," he said, his fingers caressing her cheek. "And I think we should try to make it back to the guest house. There's this nice big bathtub and . . ."

Diana stretched and rubbed against his furry chest, wishing she could purr like a cat. "Oh, I like the way you think."

"We also have a lot of plans to make. I don't want to rush you, but I don't want to spend much more time pretending that I'm not head over heels in love with you. I want to shop for an engagement ring and start making wedding plans."

Her sense of contentment ebbed slightly, but Diana held on firmly, aware that he was only facing reality. She'd promised honesty and she meant to keep that vow to him and to herself. "Can you handle a couple of more days of pretending?"

"What do you mean?"

"Maybe I'm selfish, but I'm not ready to share all this with anyone just yet and Crystal is liable to be upset, so . . ." She held her breath, not sure he'd understand why she still wasn't ready to tell Crystal.

"I doubt that Crystal will be upset by our news." His tone held an edge of amusement.

"What are you saying?"

"Either we've been careless or Crystal has a keen eye for body language. Anyway, she asked me last night if we were getting involved and I told her that I thought we might be.''

A knot tightened in her stomach. ''Was she very angry?''

''Not angry, but she did warn me that you could hurt me.'' He sighed. ''That's when I realized how much your divorce had upset her.''

''She blamed me all along. She adored Ken.''

''I think you'll find that's changed. Once I figured out what was bothering her, we had a long talk about how a marriage can look perfect on the outside and be horribly painful to the people involved. I was amazed at how well she understood. She even admitted that she resents the way Foster has treated her since the divorce.''

Hope and longing blossomed in Diana's heart. She had so missed her closeness with Crystal. ''Do you really think she would be willing to listen to my side now?''

''I know she would. And I'm sure she'll be happy for us. She wants and needs to be part of a family, Diana, and what better one could she have than sharing our joy?'' His arms tightened around her.

''Maybe we should tell her when we get back to the island.'' Her heart lifted as the last weight of sorrow fell away. ''Then she'd have time to get used to the idea before she has to go back to school.''

''I like that plan. I'm tired of hiding my feelings.'' His lips moved caressingly over hers. ''I want the whole world to know I love you and you love me.''

''And I have so many plans to make . . .'' Diana let the healing magic of his love wash over her.

''What sort of plans?'' He nibbled lightly at her neck, sending delightful chills along her nerves.

''Well, I've heard a rumor about this job opportunity in Denver and I thought I might check it out. You see, there's this great guy who lives there and . . .'' When his lips covered hers, she knew that no more words were necessary.

SHARE THE FUN . . .
SHARE YOUR NEW-FOUND TREASURE!!

You don't want to let your new books out of your sight? That's okay. Your friends can get their own. Order below.